Boise State University Western Writers Series Number 156

Reading Marilynne Robinson's *Housekeeping*

By James H. Maguire
Boise State University

Editor: Tara Penry
Editorial Assistant: Cece Gadda

Boise State University, Boise, Idaho

Library of Congress Cataloging-in-Publication Data

Maguire, James H.
Reading Marilynne Robinson's *Housekeeping* / by James H. Maguire.
p. cm. — (Boise State University western writers series ; no. 156)
Includes bibliographical references (p.) and index.
ISBN 0-88430-156-7 (pbk. : alk. paper)
1. Robinson, Marilynne. *Housekeeping*. 2. Northwestern States—In literature. I. Title. II. Series.

PS3568.O3125 H636 2003
813'.54--dc21

2002015575

Western Writers Series
English Department
Boise State University
1910 University Drive
Boise, ID 83725-1525
(208) 426-1190
wws@boisestate.edu
http://english.boisestate.edu/westernwriters

Printed in the United States of America by
Boise State University Printing and Graphic Services
Boise, Idaho

Reading Marilynne Robinson's *Housekeeping*

Reading Marilynne Robinson's *Housekeeping*

"Marilynne Robinson has written a first novel that one reads as slowly as poetry—and for the same reason: The language is so precise, so distilled, so beautiful that one doesn't want to miss any pleasure it might yield up to patience" (Schreiber 14). Many other reviewers, critics, and general readers agree with reviewer Le Anne Schreiber that Robinson's novel is beautifully written. And since *Housekeeping*'s virtual poetry echoes the beauty of the language found in works of nineteenth-century American writers such as Herman Melville and Emily Dickinson, it comes as no surprise that Robinson's favorite authors are the American Romantics.

Robinson has also stated that she sees herself as a westerner; and *Housekeeping* is set in a small northwest town similar to the ones in which the author lived as a child. At least one reviewer, Paul Gray, noted *Housekeeping*'s intense sense of place: "[. . .] the novel's vivid landscapes betray the presence of an author who lived among them [. . .]" (83). *Housekeeping*, however, does not resemble typical western American novels by men. In fact, the abandonment of women and their resulting transience—themes at the heart of *Housekeeping*—are not uniquely regional subjects. Yet in Robinson's story, the disruption of homes pushes the main characters to identify more fully with the immanent, impermanent physical world around them.

Ruth Stone, the narrator of *Housekeeping*, begins with the story of her family, starting with her maternal grandparents, Edmund and Sylvia Foster, who live in the house that Edmund builds in the town of Fingerbone. Edmund works for the railroad; and one night when he is on a train called the Fireball, returning from Spokane, he and the other hundred or so people on the train perish when it plunges into the lake near Fingerbone. The widowed Sylvia finishes raising their three daughters: sixteen-year-old Molly, fifteen-year-old Helen, and thirteen-year-old Sylvie. When the girls reach their late teens and early twenties, Molly goes to China to work for a missionary society, Helen marries Reginald Stone and sets up housekeeping in Seattle, and Sylvie, after going to Seattle to visit Helen, returns to Fingerbone only briefly to marry a man named Fisher.

Seven and a half years after Helen leaves Fingerbone, she returns with her two young daughters: Ruth and Lucille. Helen puts the girls' suitcases inside the screened porch of her mother's house, tells her daughters to wait there quietly, and then drives her car out of town and off a cliff into the lake, where she drowns.

For the next five years, their grandmother Sylvia raises her motherless granddaughters; and when she dies, two great aunts, Lily and Nona Foster, come from Spokane to take her place. The old maiden ladies find the responsibility more than they can bear, so they send for Sylvie, Helen's younger sister. Sylvie responds to their plea, and when she arrives in Fingerbone, Lily and Nona return to Spokane.

Ruth and Lucille soon discover that their aunt Sylvie has been living as a transient, and they fear she will eventually desert them when the call of the road proves too strong to keep her in Fingerbone. But Sylvie settles in to living in her childhood home and remains there even after a spring flood fills the lower floor of the house for a few days. Sylvie's "housekeeping," however, leaves the house open to the elements, and the girls roam free of supervision. Sylvie herself wanders around the countryside at all hours and often leaves Ruth and Lucille to fend for themselves.

Eventually, Lucille decides that she must leave Sylvie and Ruth so that she can receive a more normal upbringing from her Home Economics teacher. Ruth quits attending school and joins Sylvie on an outing on the lake to a ruined cabin by the shore. The good citizens of Fingerbone, concerned about Ruth's welfare, send the sheriff to let Sylvie know that she will have to surrender Ruth to the authorities. Before that can happen, Sylvie and Ruth wait until nightfall, set fire to their house, and walk over the railroad bridge that crosses the lake, the very bridge that the train plunged off when it carried Edmund Foster to his watery grave.

Ruth says that after they cross the bridge, she joins Sylvie as Sylvie resumes her life of transience. Sylvie carries a newspaper clipping that says she and Ruth died in attempting to cross the bridge, and Ruth's final words do have a proleptic tone, as if she is speaking to us from the world of the dead. Lucille, Ruth imagines, may be living in Fingerbone, or she may be in some place like Boston. Wherever she is, Ruth says, Lucille's "thoughts are thronged by our absence," although "[. . .] she does not watch, does not listen, does not wait, does not hope, and always for me and Sylvie" (219).

Such a summary of the novel is—as Susan J. Rosowski characterizes her own synopsis of *Housekeeping*—"akin to summarizing *Moby-Dick* as a man's hunt for a whale, [. . .] for it is not events but rather reflections structured as extended metaphors that make up both novels. Whereas Melville extended and pushed forward the metaphor of a hunt, Robinson extends and pushes backward the metaphor of birth until it delivers itself into a new articulation" (179). Robinson has said that she could not have written *Housekeeping* if she had not previously given birth; and many readers assume that her own life furnished the experiences that make up the novel (Rosowski 189).

Although Robinson has said that *Housekeeping* does have some autobiographical elements, she has also stated that her own childhood and adolescence were considerably different from those of Ruth and Lucille. Nevertheless, in "My Western Roots," Robinson writes of her craving for "the sort of old dull books" she found on the shelves of north Idaho: "Relevance was precisely not an issue for me: I looked to Galilee for meaning and to Spokane for orthodonture, and beyond that the world where I was I found entirely sufficient" (165). That world consisted of the towns and villages of northern Idaho and western Washington, settlements on the shores of beautiful, large lakes, surrounded by forested hills and mountains. Her paternal great-grandparents had trekked to the region in a covered wagon; and her father, John J. Summers, worked for lumber companies in the area. Her mother, Ellen Harris Summers, gave birth to Marilynne Summers in the town of Sandpoint, Idaho, on 26 November 1943.

Situated in Bonner County and on the shores of Lake Pend Oreille, Sandpoint is, as Thomas Schaub notes, "the switching yard for the three great railroads which serve the Northwest and the northern tier of the United States. Two rather long bridges cross the lake on their passage through Sandpoint. To the east of Sandpoint are the Kaniksa and Coeur d'Alene National Forests and the Bitterroot Range; Spokane, Washington is seventy miles southwest" (231). Although Robinson was born in Sandpoint, she did not grow up there, since her father's work in the lumber industry kept his family moving around the area.

Of the earliest of those years she has said:

> I spent my early, early formative period in a little non-town called Coulin, which I guess is named after those cliffs in Scotland, which was, I swear, just three houses and a store when I was a child, and this wonderful lake. And my father was always in the lumber industry and when I was very

> young he was actually sometimes a lumberjack. He was still very much in the woods then and he always came home smelling of sawdust pitch. It was very lovely. (Bartos et al. 23)

She has also said that she and her family often went to Sandpoint to spend vacations and holidays with her grandparents.

She attended high school in Coeur d'Alene, and she took a Latin class that she says had a strong influence on her style. As she explains it:

> [. . .] Mrs. Bloomsburg, my high school Latin teacher, [. . .] led five or six of us through Horace and Virgil, and taught us patience with that strange contraption called the epic simile, which, to compare great things with small, appears fairly constantly in my own prose, modified for my own purposes. It was Mrs. Bloomsburg also who trudged us through Cicero's vast sentences, clause depending from clause, the whole cantilevered with subjunctives and weighted with a culminating irony. It was all over our heads. We were bored but dogged. And at the end of it all, I think anyone can see that my style is considerably more in debt to Cicero than to Hemingway.
>
> I admire Hemingway. It is simply an amusing accident that it should be Cicero, of all people, whose influence I must resist. This befell me because I was educated at a certain time in a certain place. When I went to college in New England I found that only I and a handful of boys prepared by the Jesuits shared these quaint advantages. In giving them to Ruth I used her to record the intellectual culture of the West as I experienced it myself. ("My Western Roots" 167)

Brown University in Rhode Island is the New England college that Robinson attended from 1962 until her graduation in 1966.

During her freshman year, her older brother, David, was also at Brown and was a senior studying art and art history. She majored in English, taking courses in American literature and in religious studies. When she took a creative writing course taught by novelist John Hawkes, he defended her Ciceronian style when her classmates attacked it.

Following her graduation from Brown in 1966, Robinson entered the graduate program in English at the University of Washington; and from 1966 to 1970, she held a National Defense Education Act Fellowship. While in graduate school, she married and had two sons, James and Joseph. In 1969, she received her M.A.; and she earned her doctorate in 1977 with a dissertation titled "A New Look at Shakespeare's *Henry VI, Part II*: Sources, Structure and Meaning." In recommending that the dissertation be accepted, her reading committee gave her a strong commendation: "[. . .] Mrs. Robinson uses traditional methods of literary criticism; what is unusual here is not only the play to which she applies them, but the sensitivity with which she has used them to arrive at an excellently written and most perceptive dissertation from which Shakespeareans cannot but learn" ("A New Look" n.p.).

While still at work on her dissertation, Robinson had written the opening of *Housekeeping*. In Rennes, France, as a visiting professor at the Université de Haute Bretagne for academic year 1978-79, she resumed work on the novel. She says that once it was completed, she had no trouble finding a publisher. In 1981, *Housekeeping* was published by Farrar, Straus, Giroux and received considerable acclaim. Robinson then began writing a second novel (still to be published) as well as essays and book reviews for publications such as the *New York Times* and *Harper's*.

During the 1980s, she served as a writer in residence or a visiting professor at Washington University in St. Louis (spring 1983), at the University of Kent in England (1983-84), at the Fine Arts

Center in Provincetown, Massachusetts (January 1984), at Amherst College (1985-86), at the University of Massachusetts (fall 1987), and at the University of Alabama (spring 1988). Also during the eighties, she began to write about the pumping of radioactive waste into the Irish Sea from a British nuclear reprocessing plant called Sellafield. After she first expressed her concerns about Sellafield in essays and letters published in *Harper's*, her detailed exposé of this contamination of the ocean was published in book form in 1989 under the title *Mother Country*. Although the book met with a mixed response from reviewers, it was a finalist for the National Book Award in 1989.

Because she had criticized Greenpeace in *Mother Country*, the environmental group brought what proved to be a successful lawsuit for libel against Robinson's British publisher. As a result of the ruling against her publisher, *Mother Country* was banned in Great Britain. The lawsuit came at a bad time for Robinson, since she and her husband had separated in 1989 and she was raising their two sons on her own. She began teaching in the New York State Writers Program at Skidmore College; and since the spring of 1991, she has taught at the University of Iowa as a member of the faculty of the Writers' Workshops. Her collection *The Death of Adam: Essays on Modern Thought* was published by Houghton Mifflin in 1998 and, like *Mother Country*, was praised for its style, although not all reviewers agreed with Robinson's controversial thesis "that the prevailing view of things can be assumed to be wrong, and that its opposite, being its image or shadow, can also be assumed to be wrong" (1).

In reaching no consensus about the value and validity of Robinson's views and ideas, reviewers are not alone. On one point, however, a near consensus has been reached by reviewers, general readers, and critics: namely, that Robinson writes powerfully, evocatively, and beautifully. Amidst the acclaim and controversy, in the first two decades following *Housekeeping*'s publication, more than seventy critical articles, book chapters, doctoral dissertations, and master's theses have been written about the novel (not to mention more than fifteen interviews conducted with Robinson, in most of which she discusses *Housekeeping*); and most of these literary assessments illuminate at least some facet of Robinson's art. Lisa Durose's "Marilynne Robinson: A Bibliography" gives a listing of all the criticism published by the mid 1990s.

The critics examine *Housekeeping*'s characters, themes, subjects, imagery, symbols, and ideas. They look at the differences between Sylvie and her mother, Ruth and Lucille, and the women and men in the novel. They explore how Ruth's story dramatizes the tensions between civilization and nature, society and the individual, conformity and nonconformity, confinement and freedom, appearance and reality, and stasis and change. Critics also discuss the novel's water imagery and the symbolic use of the natural setting—the lake, the forests, and the mountains. Ideas about the nature of the home, of the self, and of community also figure prominently in scholarly studies of *Housekeeping*.

All this criticism defies useful categorization because so many of these studies take more than one approach to the novel or focus on more than one issue. Nevertheless, five general areas of critical concern can be discerned: 1) the nature and lives of women as distinct from men; 2) the relationship between humans and the natural world; 3) intertextual studies that focus on the connections between *Housekeeping* and earlier works of literary art such as those by the American Romantics; 4) the novel's exploration of the issues of transience, homelessness, and abandonment; and 5) consideration of *Housekeeping* as a novel of the American west.

In the reading of *Housekeeping* that follows, I will draw upon much of the criticism in order to explain the novel and to support my view that it is a western American version of the Book of

Ruth. Although the following reading will examine the novel chapter by chapter, readers should keep in mind that, as Christine Caver has pointed out, *Housekeeping* has three parts: "Ruth's narrative of her family's history and dynamics, which conveys as much by what she leaves unsaid as by what she records [chapters one through three]; Ruth's and Lucille's diverging paths after Sylvie's arrival [chapters four through seven]; and Ruth's final transformation as she enters into Sylvie's world [chapters eight through eleven]" (118). Moreover, all of *Housekeeping*'s chapters have a number of sections, indicated by extra space between paragraphs. The number and length of the sections affect the narrative pace and rhythm, among other functions. Chapter one has eight sections; chapter two has two; chapter three has three; chapter four has three; chapter five has four; chapter six has two; chapter seven has five; chapter eight has three; chapter nine has three; chapter ten has two; and chapter eleven has three.

Since the novel's title appears before any of the chapters and sections, a reading of *Housekeeping* should begin by explaining the significance of the title. As Tace Hedrick has noted, "The novel plays on the notion of the word *to keep*, which itself comes from the Anglo-Saxon *cepan*, to behold, to watch out for, as well as to lay hold of, akin to the Indo-European base *gab*, which is to *look* at or for" (142). As a number of critics have pointed out, Robinson presents the novel's readers with a strong irony when Sylvie and Ruth "keep" their house by setting fire to it and leaving it. The narrative prepares us for that irony, as Heather Bohannan explains, since "Nature and culture coincide in the symbol of house and housekeeping, for Sylvie reverses inside and outside—allowing leaves and small animals to drift into the house, leaving the lights off during meals until the darkness inside and out is one and the same, letting the davenport molder in the yard" (73).

Sylvie's bizarre domestic practices subvert the cultural norms that are the basis for consumer publications such as *Good Housekeeping*. Moreover, as George Toles explains, "To keep house in nature means, above all, to give up all rights (and thoughts) of ownership. Leave the house as open as possible to the elements, so that the house does not come to seem a barrier to Being" (150). Even in nature the house poses dangers since, as Siân Mile puts it, "For Robinson, the house is a bar to subjectivity because it consumes the subject" (132). Robinson may see the house as having such power because, as Paula Geyh argues, "[S]ubjectivity and space are mutually constructing: while subjects constitute themselves through the creation of spaces, these same spaces also elicit and structure subjectivities" (104).

If all that seems to place too much importance on a one-word title, consider a statement that Robinson made in an interview with Tace Hedrick:

> I used to say to myself that *Walden* could have been called *Housekeeping*. It seems to me that in *Walden*, Thoreau is trying to create, in terms of physical existence, in terms of food and shelter, a life, a physical life in the world that is both minimal and optimum. It's the reduction of being to essentials with the assumption that this kind of reduction is an enhancement. (Bartos et al. 4)

Robinson has also stated in a number of interviews, essays, and reviews that she admires not only Henry David Thoreau but also other great writers of the American Renaissance, including Ralph Waldo Emerson, Emily Dickinson, Herman Melville, and Edgar Allan Poe. Indeed, she adds that she considers her own writing the resumption of a conversation begun by them.

Given that Thoreau and his peers focus on houses and housekeeping as metaphors and symbols, Robinson's choice of a title indicates a similar purpose. William Burke, at any rate, argues that "the novel's title [. . .] suggests that house-keeping may be seen as spirit-keeping in its earthly forms" (720). At the same time, as Joan Kirkby points out, "Housekeeping [. . .] becomes a metaphor for Art, all the various human contrivances and constructs by which we attempt to stay the inexorable forces of decay, the unregulated energies of nature. Of course this is what ordinary housekeeping is about too, stemming the forces of decay, the fresh ravages that each new day brings" (93).

Any readers who overlook the significance of *Housekeeping*'s title soon have another chance to recognize that Robinson's novel is profound and polysemous, for its first sentence contains an allusion to the Bible: "My name is Ruth" (3). Although it is one of the shortest books of the Old Testament, the Book of Ruth is also one of the most memorable. It tells the story of Ruth, a Moabitess who marries one of the two sons of Naomi, a woman who has come from Bethlehem with her family to dwell in Moab. When Naomi's husband and two sons die, she tells Ruth and Orpah (her other daughter-in-law) that they should return to their mothers' houses. Orpah does eventually go back to her mother, but Ruth says:

> Intreat me not to leave thee, or to return from following after thee: for whither thou goest, I will go; and where thou lodgest, I will lodge: thy people shall be my people, and thy God my God. Where thou diest, will I die, and there will I be buried: the Lord do so to me, and more also, if ought but death part thee and me. (Ruth 1: 16-17)

Then Naomi allows Ruth to accompany her when she returns to Bethlehem, where she recognizes Boaz, one of her husband's kinsmen. Ruth receives Naomi's permission to glean in Boaz's field; and when he notices Ruth among the other gleaners, he tells her to continue gleaning in his field and he praises her for her selfless devotion to Naomi. Hearing of the favor Boaz has shown Ruth, Naomi tells her daughter-in-law to go again to Boaz's field, stay after nightfall and wait until he lies down to sleep, and then to uncover his legs and lie down beside him. Ruth does as Naomi has instructed her, and when Boaz wakes and finds Ruth lying beside him, he tells her that he will arrange for her redemption (i.e., marriage).

As it happens, Boaz himself marries Ruth. The witnesses at the wedding say to Boaz: "The Lord make the woman that is come into thine house like Rachel and like Leah, which two did build the house of Israel" (Ruth 4: 11). In due course, Ruth gives birth to a son who will provide for Naomi in her old age and who will beget Jesse, the father of David. When Ruth's son is born, the women say to Naomi: "Blessed be the Lord, which hath not left thee this day without a kinsman, that his name may be famous in Israel. And he shall be unto thee a restorer of thy life, and a nourisher of thine old age: for thy daughter in law, which loveth thee, which is better to thee than seven sons, hath born him" (Ruth 4: 14-15).

Unlike the Ruth of the Bible, Ruth Stone does not marry; and Robinson's Ruth chooses to leave all for her aunt, not for a mother-in-law. Given such differences, readers might wonder whether Robinson intended the allusion. In her interview with Tace Hedrick, she said:

> The name Ruth has such powerful suggestions for me. I know that simply making the choice of the narrator's name was important—which was a thing that I did very early—having to do with pity and grief and compassion and also vulnerability. I mean, again, feeding from the Book of Ruth itself rather than just the meaning of the name. The Book of Ruth was the name suggested to me by people who read the book, but that didn't seem appropriate.

> The issue in the Book of Ruth—the question is—who to follow. And the decision that Ruth makes is, "Where thou goest I shall go; thy people shall be my people and thy God, my God." It seems to me that in a certain way the Ruth in my book makes that kind of radical choice about whose terms of reality will she accept. When she follows Sylvie, she's passing from one civilization to another. (2)

Another strong similarity between the two Ruths is the love that moves them to remain the companions of homeless women who face uncertain futures. And, as Ilana Pardes has noted, "The Book of Ruth is the only biblical text in which the word 'love' is used to define a relationship between two women" (102).

A number of critics have commented on the significance of *Housekeeping*'s allusion to the Book of Ruth. Anne-Marie Mallon, for example, writes:

> The Book of Ruth provides an important touchstone for Robinson and her readers as we struggle to re-envision the terms and designs of dispossession. It ties the novel to a tradition of storytelling that speaks for fulfillment in the midst of wandering; and it links Ruth to a woman whose refusal to stay safely home is a pledge of faith in the endurance of the human spirit and the human family. (96)

Mallon adds, however, that "We do not easily accept the resonance, perhaps because women, more so than men, are bound by conventions dictated by an impressive, yet repressive, series of unargued domestic equations: woman is the heart of the home; home is where the heart is; woman is the homemaker and housekeeper" (96). Although we may agree with Mallon about our resistance to the resonance of the allusion, we can also recognize that, like the nineteenth-century American authors Robinson emulates, she challenges unexamined convention relentlessly.

One of the conventional views that comes under siege in *Housekeeping* is the belief that transience is unacceptable as a way of life. Maggie Galehouse argues that by

> [r]efashioning some of the standard associations of the transient or hobo, *Housekeeping* portrays drifting as a kind of liberation, an unencumbering, a casting-off of unnecessary objects and social responsibilities. Robinson narrates transience in a number of ways: *formally*, via Ruth's first-person narration and by borrowing the frame and tone of a well-known biblical tale; *historically*, by giving the novel a rural, post-Depression setting; *physically*, by generating a dialogue between indoors and outdoors; and *temporally*, by endowing her main characters with an alinear conception of time, and, in turn, reimagining their relationship to objects of containment, such as houses and clothing. (119)

Clearly, the title and first sentence of *Housekeeping* reflect on every other part of the novel.

We have not yet, however, considered the full significance of *Housekeeping*'s opening sentence: "My name is Ruth" (3). That statement alludes not only to the Book of Ruth but also to Herman Melville's *Moby-Dick*. In her interview with Tace Hedrick, Robinson said: "Frankly, when I wrote that first sentence, what I was specifically thinking of was 'Call me Ishmael' [the opening line of the narrative part of *Moby-Dick*]" (6). Hedrick had asked about the resemblance between *Housekeeping*'s first sentence and the opening of Edgar Allan Poe's *Narrative of A. Gordon Pym*; and after Robinson said she had been thinking of *Moby-Dick* instead, she added:

> But I think Melville might very well have been thinking of "My name is Arthur Gordon Pym." *Arthur Gordon Pym* and *Moby-Dick* have the same—and for that matter, *Huckleberry*

> *Finn*—have that characteristic pattern of so much American literature where people go through a journey that leads to a kind of realization that is just at the limits of their ability to comprehend or articulate, and after that, there's an openness where earlier experience becomes impossible, and you're abandoned into a new terrain without being able to use your old assumptions about how to find your way. (6)

Like *Housekeeping*'s opening line, "Call me Ishmael" also alludes to the Bible. In the Book of Genesis, Ishmael is the son fathered by Abraham and born of Hagar, the Egyptian maid of Sarah, Abraham's wife. When Hagar, newly pregnant with Ishmael, had fled from the wrath of Sarah, an angel of the Lord had appeared to her and proclaimed: "Behold, thou art with child, and shalt bear a son, and shalt call his name Ishmael; because the Lord hath heard thy affliction. And he will be a wild man; his hand will be against every man, and every man's hand against him; and he shall dwell in the presence of all his brethren" (Genesis 16: 11-12). But as Christopher Sten points out, "'Ishmael' is not the given name of Melville's narrator; it is the name he appropriates for himself after the fact, because it so aptly captures his experience as a castaway who in the end finds the Father after all" (216).

Ruth Stone does not appropriate her name as Melville's Ishmael does his, but she, too, is a castaway. And like Ishmael, Ruth shares with her readers her meditations on life and death, illusion and reality, loss and restoration. In addition to Ishmael's account of some of his own life, *Moby-Dick* also includes stories of orphans such as Pip and lost children such as the son of the captain of the *Rachel*; and Ruth, her sister, and her aunts are also virtual orphans and lost children. Although no Captain Ahab plays a part in *Housekeeping*, Robinson's novel resembles *Moby-Dick* in giving readers the means to discover "something of our deeper selves," as Sten puts it. Both novels are, as Sten says of Melville's masterpiece, religious texts (216). Such an assertion is not, of course, proven by the title and first sentence of the novel. Nevertheless, carefully considered, *Housekeeping*'s title and initial statement alert us to the likelihood that what follows will prove to be much more than anything merely mundane.

After Ruth introduces herself, she gives the names of members of her family. Having noticed the significance of Ruth's name, many critics and readers have also found significant meanings in the names of Ruth's family members. *Lucille*, for example, derives from Latin words having to do with light: "bright, shining, transparent." Lucille Stone prefers the lighted houses of Fingerbone's conventional citizens to the unlighted house that Sylvie keeps. *Sylvia* comes from the Latin *sylva*, meaning "woods." Sylvie's name fits her, since she roams for hours through the woods and opens the family's house to the natural elements and the creatures of the forest. Joan Kirkby says that "Ruthie's guide on the journey to the Great Mother ["not sentimentalized 'Mother Nature' but the inexorable non-human figure of Jungian mythology, the great mother associated with the dark primeval water, the swamp, 'the fertile muck'" (101)] is Aunt Sylvie, an almost Spenserian evocation of the goddess of mutability" (102).

The name *Foster* suggests nurturing, but it also brings to mind "foster child" and "orphan." After the death of Edmund Foster, his daughters go through life as if they had been orphaned by his death, even though his wife survived him. *Fisher*, the name of Sylvie's husband, conjures up images of people seeking food out in the elements and in a way not much different from how other animals find something to eat. Ruth and Lucille's two great-aunts, Lily and Nona Foster, also have significant names. *Lily* is like one of the "lilies of the field" mentioned in the Bible: they neither toil nor spin. *Nona* sounds like a word related to *nonentity*. Certainly the two great-aunts in *Housekeeping* seem little more than helpless nonentities sustained by a merciful Providence. Finally, Robinson may have picked at random *Edmund* as the first name of Ruth's grandfather, or she may have had in mind some of Shakespeare's Edmunds, with their associations with doom.

Edmund Foster's doom is, in a way, reminiscent of the disasters visited upon biblical characters such as Job and Jonah, although Foster drowns whereas Job and Jonah survive God's infliction of catastrophe upon them. Ruth tells us about Edmund's penchant for travel literature and about his paintings of mountains. These interests spark his urge for westering and prompt him to take his wife to Fingerbone. Of his artistry, Ruth writes: "Whether the genius of this painting was ignorance or fancy I never could decide" (4). Historians have been similarly perplexed in trying to determine whether westering, the force that led to the settlement of the American west, derived its power from ignorance or fancy. Like the Joads in John Steinbeck's *The Grapes of Wrath* (another western American novel with strong parallels to a book in the Bible—namely, Exodus), the Fosters are representative, an Everyman and his wife, daughters, and granddaughters. When the Fireball, with Edmund aboard, plunges into the lake, his wife and daughters experience the sense of abandonment felt by many among the first several generations of the west's European American women. As Ruth sees it, Edmund's death "had troubled the very medium of their lives" (15).

In describing the town, the lake, and their surroundings, Ruth reveals a western American sensibility that is also discernible in the works of the west's best authors. She writes:

> The terrain on which the town itself is built is relatively level, having once belonged to the lake. It seems there was a time when the dimensions of things modified themselves, leaving a number of puzzling margins, as between the mountains as they must have been and the mountains as they are

> now, or between the lake as it once was and the lake as it is now. (5)

That awareness of geologic forces situates the narrative in geologic time, just as it is also situated in historic time by references to matters that place most of the story in a post-Depression, pre-1960s timeframe. We find a similar cognizance of geologic time in well-known poems by westerners; some good examples are Robinson Jeffers' "Continent's End," Thomas Hornsby Ferril's "Time of Mountains," and Gary Snyder's "Endless Streams and Mountains." Seeing humans in the context of geologic time on an Earth regarded as sacred gives the land spiritual value and a role in the human drama that unfolds in western American literature.

Moreover, as Susan J. Rosowski points out:

> Robinson's composition of place also fulfills an epistemological function in that she conceives of the lake as a symbol so powerful that it functions in her narrative as a gravitational field to which the characters, the plot, and language itself are attracted. Fragmented and multiple images collapse into one another as if pulled downward and inward toward their genesis, and genesis itself is returned to its Latin and Greek meanings of generation, origin, and birth. (182)

Those collapsing images form only one of the novel's narrative patterns, however.

Beginning with Edmund's death, *Housekeeping*'s drama also includes repetitions, just as events in the Bible replicate in ways that build meaning by comparison and contrast and by the force of accumulation. The first repetition in *Housekeeping* occurs near the end of the first chapter, when Helen's suicidal plunge into the lake repeats the fatal plunge of the Fireball with her father on it. Ruth's account of her mother's suicide presents it matter-of-factly, as if it were almost commonplace. The reader must infer that

Helen feels, in her sense of abandonment and despair, that her grief can be assuaged only by a suicide patterned on her father's death. After Helen's suicide, her mother repeats the pattern of raising her daughters by beginning to raise her granddaughters: "[. . .] she whited shoes and braided hair and turned back bedclothes as if re-enacting the commonplace would make it merely commonplace again [. . .]" (25). By re-occuring, the patterns in the lives of the Fosters and their daughters and granddaughters come to seem portentous and prophetic, like the succession of types and anti-types in the Old and New Testaments.

Chapter two provides a contrast to, and comic relief from, the disasters of the first chapter. Sylvia Foster dies peacefully—as Ruth puts it, "[. . .] my grandmother one winter morning eschewed awakening [. . .]" (29)—and her sisters-in-law, Lily and Nona Foster, come from Spokane to care for Ruth and Lucille. Several long passages in the chapter consist of nothing but dialogue between the two great-aunts, conversations that go nowhere. Yet the two old women never quit talking as they go about their almost ritualistic routines. Rosowski notes that "[. . .] Ruth's two great-aunts appear as female versions of [Samuel] Beckett's Gogo and Didi [in *Waiting for Godot*] in that they serve as a narrative bridge by creating an awareness of need—an existential gap, one might say" (179). Their speech and actions also bear a striking resemblance to those of Nagg and Nell (in Beckett's *Endgame* [1958]), two peevish characters whose existence consists of waiting for death to arrive. Lily and Nona do little but await death, too; and what remains of their lives is tightly circumscribed by their compulsive devotion to domestic routines. Ruth says: "Lily and Nona, I think, enjoyed nothing except habit and familiarity, the precise replication of one day in the next" (32). If we see them as laughable role models, then surely Ruth makes a wise choice in avoiding a mode of being that leads to a living entombment in the comforts of conventionality.

Whatever their merits as role models, Lily and Nona endure the stresses of parenting for little more than a season before they send a cry for help to Sylvie. Before Sylvie's return, the great-aunts discuss their sister-in-law's obituary, "which was considered an impressive tribute to her," Ruth tells us, "and was expected to be a source of pride to us" (41). It proves to be quite the opposite, however. As Ruth puts it:

> I was simply alarmed. It suggested to me that the earth had opened. In fact, I dreamed that I was walking across the ice on the lake, which was breaking up as it does in the spring, softening and shifting and pulling itself apart. But in the dream the surface that I walked on proved to be knit up of hands and arms and upturned faces [. . .]. (41)

The strange dream, Ruth adds, made her think that her grandmother "had entered into some other element upon which our lives floated as weightless, intangible, immiscible, and inseparable as reflections in water" (41). The surreal quality of Ruth's dream gives her a sense that the worlds of both the living and the dead share a similar surreal nature. Even before Sylvie arrives on the scene, therefore, we can see that Ruth has started to see life and death in ways that are unusual and highly unconventional.

At the start of chapter three, when Sylvie arrives, she enters the house quietly, but her appearance blazons her transient lifestyle:

> Her hair was wet, her hands were red and withered from the cold, her feet were bare except for loafers. Her raincoat was so shapeless and oversized that she must have found it on a bench. (45)

Next morning, Sylvie leaves the house before anyone else is up, and when Ruth and Lucille discover that she's gone, they also leave the house, hoping to find her and to keep her with them in

Fingerbone. She does return to the house with the girls; and later, when Lucille asks Sylvie to describe their mother, Sylvie excuses her poor attempt to do so by saying, "It's hard to describe someone you know so well" (51). Because Sylvie reminds Ruth of her mother more and more, she says that "[. . .] Sylvie began to blur the memory of my mother, and then to displace it" (53). Then Ruth tries to excuse Sylvie's failure to describe Helen. Reticence didn't keep Sylvie from giving a better description. Instead, Ruth says, "[. . .] memories are by their nature fragmented, isolated, and arbitrary as glimpses one has at night through lighted windows" (53).

Ruth, however, seems to the reader to have no trouble describing people, and her memories do not seem "fragmented, isolated, and arbitrary." Her defense of Sylvie must arise from a need to justify the aunt who has taken the place of her mother and who is not only kin but kindred spirit. Lucille, on the other hand, has little in common with Sylvie, although Lucille lies to Lily and Nona in a desperate attempt to insure that Sylvie will stay. We can see that Sylvie seldom bothers to dissemble and that she does not share Lucille's dependence on others. Lucille's lie convinces Lily and Nona that Sylvie can be relied upon to care responsibly for the girls, whereupon the great-aunts waste no time in departing for Spokane; and with their departure, the third chapter ends.

In *Housekeeping*'s fourth chapter, Ruth gives an account of the flood that submerges most of the town of Fingerbone within a few weeks of Sylvie's return. A three-day thaw and a four-day rain precipitate the flooding. Sylvie, Lucille, and Ruth watch and listen silently to the sights and sounds of the flooding lake. As Rosowski observes, this repetition "of the biblical flood provides an exercise in hearing silence" (182); and she adds that "To hear silence is to experience the reduction of self to intuition, a return to origins, and an intension of meaning—the passage prepares for the experience of *Housekeeping* more broadly" (183). During the thaw, Ruth and Lucille make a snow sculpture that looks like a woman standing in a cold wind. In her forlornness, the snow woman symbolizes the bereft and abandoned women of Ruth's family. And when Sylvie tries to tell the girls about how loneliness bothers some people, the snow woman comes to mind. Sylvie, however, doesn't mind being alone, an attitude that Robinson says is characteristic of many westerners ("My Western Roots" 167). Lucille, on the other hand, clearly does dislike lonesomeness, and Sylvie can see that that's how her niece feels about it.

Besides accentuating their loneliness, the flood keeps Ruth and Lucille in such close proximity to Sylvie for such an extended period that the girls can't fail to observe unmistakable signs of their aunt's eccentric behavior. At the same time, Ruth's meditations imply that the isolation created by the flood, added to the subversion of the "normal" caused by Sylvie's behavior, leads her to an introspection that eventually results in her choice of transience rather than a fixed domesticity. When Ruth tells us that "Every spirit passing through the world fingers the tangible and mars the mutable, and finally has come to look and not to buy" (73), she expresses not only the belief that guides her decision to join Sylvie in a life of transience but also one of the main themes of *Housekeeping*. It is also one of the main themes of most of the masterpieces of the American Renaissance.

Chapter four calls to mind not only the American Romantics but also the story of Noah and the flood in the Bible's Book of Genesis. Later in her narrative, Ruth shares more of her thoughts about Noah and his wife, and we will consider those in due course. For now, readers should notice that the Fingerbone flood ushers in spring, with its associations of cleansing and renewal. Ironically, for Sylvie, Ruth, and Lucille, the flood, by bringing the lake into their house, provides a dramatic reminder of their family's past, specifically the drowning of Edmund and Helen. Yet because their house stands on a hill and escapes the worst of the flooding, the townspeople regard Sylvie and her nieces as unscathed: "Two weeks after the water was gone people began to believe that our house had not been touched by the flood at all" (75).

Chapter five begins after the flood has receded and the mud has been shoveled away. Ruth and Lucille resume their attendance at Fingerbone's junior high school, "named for William Henry Harrison" (76). The ninth president of the United States, Harrison died of pneumonia after serving only one month in office. His unremarkable position among the presidents matches Fingerbone's status among other communities. And since Harrison earned the nickname "Tippecanoe" by defeating the Shawnee Indians at the Battle of Tippecanoe, the pun in naming a lakeside institution after him makes it seem comically inappropriate. Nothing is comical, however, about Ruth and Lucille's typical adolescent shyness. Ruth says that at lunchtime, "[. . .] we stood apart and hugged our ribs, and looked back over our shoulders" (76).

Their classes, unfortunately, offer no compensatory satisfactions. Instead, "Hours of tedium were relieved by occasional minor humiliations [. . .]" (76). Ruth gives a few specific examples of these "minor humiliations," including the following: "Once I was required to stand by my desk and recite 'I Heard a Fly Buzz When I Died'" (76-77). The poem Ruth has to recite is by Emily Dickinson, one of American literature's major authors. Ruth's familiarity with Dickinson's work explains why Ruth's narrative contains images, metaphors, and a point of view strikingly like those found in Dickinson's poetry. Indeed, so striking is the resemblance that Thomas Gardner argues: "What *Housekeeping* does is very simple: it picks up on a set of images and situations first put into play by Emily Dickinson and unfolds them in a new situation, examining the world they make visible" (11). Gardner bases his argument not only on Ruth's mention of the Dickinson poem but also on Robinson's statements in "My Western Roots" that "*Housekeeping* is meant as a sort of demonstration of the intellectual culture of my childhood"; and that "Emily Dickinson and the Bible were blessedly unavoidable" (166).

The source of Ruth's way of looking at her homelessness Gardner locates in Dickinson's "In Many and Reportless Places," a poem in which the speaker says that departing joy sometimes "leaves a sumptuous Destitution" (Gardner 12). The joy cannot be rediscovered by searching, since it "has no home"; and it leaves homeless and roaming those who have "once inhaled it." Gardner says that "[. . .] Ruth's tale of how she became a homeless, lyric-voiced drifter [. . .]" is a "detailed fleshing out" of "In Many and Reportless Places." He adds that

> [. . .] Ruth's account of what is sumptuous about destitution not only unfolds Dickinson's analogy of wandering without an established home, it also extends Dickinson's way of speaking, as in a conversation in which the gestures and intonations of one participant are reflected and varied and tested in those of another. (12)

When Ruth and Dickinson narrate tales of "sumptuous Destitution," they are, as the poet Richard Wilbur says of Dickinson, "simply describing the way things go in the human soul, telling us that the frustration of appetite awakens or abets desire, and that the effect of intense desiring is to render any finite satisfaction disappointing" (56-57).

Although I agree with Gardner's view that Ruth often extends Dickinson's way of speaking, I do not agree that "What *Housekeeping* does is very simple [. . .]." Robinson employs Dickinson's rhetoric within a larger framework that Susan Rosowski has identified as the tradition of meditative poetry.

Louis Martz, as Rosowski explains, has defined the meditative poem as "a work that creates an interior drama of the mind [. . .]" (Rosowski 179). Such dramas usually have three acts: "a threefold meditative structure of memory, analysis, and understanding [. . .]" (180). The three acts typically conclude with a colloquy, a conversation between the self and God. Rosowski says that for Robinson the colloquy "takes the form of the self in conversation with the landscape" (180).

Ruth usually finds the landscape more accessible than are any of her adult relatives. Her mother commits suicide when Ruth is still a young girl. Her grandmother dies during the first years of Ruth's adolescence. Her aunt Sylvie seems preoccupied and ready to revert to a life of transience. Then, when the humiliation of being accused of cheating drives Lucille from perfect school attendance to playing hooky by the lakeshore, Ruth accompanies her, and the girls watch aghast one afternoon as Sylvie walks out on the railroad bridge into a strong wind. It is as if Sylvie wants to know what the transit from life to death was like for her father and sister and so ventures dangerously close to drowning herself. When she sees her nieces watching her, she returns to the shore; and when Lucille says, "If you fell in, everyone would think you did it on purpose [. . .]" (82), Sylvie tries to reassure the girls. But Ruth writes: "We were very upset, all the same, for reasons too numerous to mention. Clearly our aunt was not a stable person" (82).

The girls' fears keep them apprehensively watching Sylvie's every move for several days. What they fear is that Sylvie will go too far in trying to share the experience of her father's and sister's last moments. As Ruth expresses it:

> [I]magine that same Sylvie trudging up from the lake bottom, foundered coat and drowned sleeves and marbled lips and marble fingers and eyes flooded with the deep water that gleamed down beneath the reach of light. She might

very well have said: "I've always wondered what that would be like." (84)

Instead of the wry speaker of Dickinson's proleptic "I Heard a Fly Buzz When I Died," Sylvie becomes, in Ruth's fearful vision, like a character from one of Edgar Allan Poe's tales about women who return from the dead.

As Gardner points out, in conjuring up such a hypothetical vision of a drowned Sylvie, Ruth uses a speculative analogy like the ones Emily Dickinson uses in her poetry (Gardner 16). By getting us to think of situations that don't exist but that are similar to ones that do, the two authors awaken us to possibilities that lie just outside the actual and the ordinary. Gardner says that Ruth's narrative uses this technique "by unfolding, throughout the length of the novel, a series of analogies based on the spectacular derailment of her grandfather's train years before she was born" (17). There are, in fact, two dozen of these hypothetical scenes in *Housekeeping*. Most chapters include only one or two of them. Chapter five, for example, has, in addition to the passage in which Ruth asks us to imagine a drowned Sylvie, an imaginary scene featuring Ruth's aunt Molly.

What prompts the scene with Molly is a missionary brochure that Ruth finds in her grandmother's house. The brochure includes, in italics, Christ's statement to His apostles: "*I will make you fishers of men*" (91). That statement becomes linked, in Ruth's mind, to her aunt Molly's departure and her grandfather's drowning. Ruth writes: "Even now I always imagine her leaning from the low side of some small boat, dropping her net through the spumy billows of the upper air" (91). The net, as Ruth's mind continues to speculate, would sweep up all the people on earth and then all those drowned in the lake near Fingerbone, including her mother and (though she does not mention him) her grandfather, too. This reverie arises, Ruth says, "perhaps only from watching gulls fly like sparks up the face of clouds [. . .]"; but as a way of finding a reason for the sort of "general rescue" she has imagined, it leads her to state "a law of completion—that everything must finally be made comprehensible [. . .]" (92).

As we will see when we come to chapters eight and eleven, the number of such hypothetical scenes increases as Ruth's emotions intensify and as she tries to explain how ordinary-appearing events come to seem wonderful and miraculous to her.

By the end of chapter five, Sylvie's behavior strikes Lucille as being anything but wonderful. Although Ruth says that she "was content with Sylvie," she finds "advantage in conforming my attitudes to [Lucille's]. She was of the common persuasion" (92-93). Clearly, however, Ruth follows Lucille's lead only because of the advantage of appearing to be "of the common persuasion." The differences between Sylvie and Lucille have become unmistakable. Ruth says of Lucille: "Time that had not come yet—an anomaly in itself—had the fiercest reality for her" (93). In contrast, "Sylvie, on her side, inhabited a millennial present" (94).

In chapter six, Ruth gains some sense of that millennial present during what she says is "perhaps the first true summer of my life" (95). She and Lucille add April and May to the summer by ceasing to attend school after the end of March. During the months of April and May, the girls don school clothes and head off to school each day, but then they follow railroad tracks to the lake and the railroad bridge. Ruth tells us that "The hoboes built on the shore in the bridge's very shadows" (95). Since their grandmother had warned the girls "that hoboes made a practice of whisking children under their coats and carrying them off" (95-96), Ruth and Lucille only look from a distance at the hoboes near the bridge.

Maggie Galehouse says that "Sylvie shares with the hoboes and migrant workers of that time a mania for mobility, riding the boxcars and finding work when and where she can. Yet she also stands outside some of the standard associations regarding the female hobo" (125). Ruth, however, does not mention Sylvie's resemblance to the hoboes; and, as Galehouse adds, Sylvie does not share the female hobo's sexual aura, nor does she choose drifting "as much as it chooses her, since no other lifestyle is better suited to her actions and temperament" (125). Nevertheless, the citizens of Fingerbone clearly see Sylvie as a hobo or at least a recovering hobo. And, as Galehouse says, "Whether it is promiscuity, or class, or both, female hoboes threaten the status quo by reminding the nontransient population that women can and do exist outside the polarities of prostitution and domesticity, and that many women might find themselves, given a certain set of circumstances, sleeping in boxcars" (125).

Seeing the hoboes by the railroad bridge evokes from Ruth another speculative analogy in which she imagines that she and Lucille and the hoboes "might have escaped the destruction of some sleek train [. . .]" (96). There, by the lakeside, the survivors would witness the resurrection of her grandfather and the other passengers who were on the Fireball, and the resurrection would also include her grandmother and her mother. That the sight of hoboes can evoke from Ruth such an imagined scene shows that the orphaned girl's feelings of loss and abandonment are powerfully stirred by seeing people like her aunt Sylvie near the site of her grandfather's and mother's drownings. Ruth's emotional tumult here joins an accumulating body of evidence that she and Lucille and Sylvie have been traumatized by parental deaths. That growing evidence becomes unavoidable in the last four chapters of the novel.

For the remainder of the summer (and for the rest of chapter six), however, Ruth and Lucille continue playing in the woods during the day and sitting with Sylvie in the darkness after nightfall. The girls find the woods disturbing, and an old quarry with a cave and a mine is, for them, "a great and attractive terror" (97). Nevertheless, in a sentence whose beginning echoes a statement in Henry David Thoreau's *Walden*, Ruth writes, "[. . .] I went to the woods for the woods' own sake, while, increasingly, Lucille seemed to be enduring a banishment there" (99). Lucille accepts exile in the woods because it takes her away from Sylvie's bizarre attempts to keep house.

Believing that fresh air provides the best means of housekeeping, Sylvie leaves open the doors and windows of her mother's house. As Ruth wryly puts it, "Sylvie in a house was more or less like a mermaid in a ship's cabin. She preferred it sunk in the very element it was meant to exclude" (99). Sylvie's approach to housekeeping resembles Thoreau's; and Tace Hedrick says Robinson told her "that in writing *Housekeeping*, she had *Walden* 'very much in mind'" (140). Hedrick sees Sylvie as being "in a very real sense, the Thoreauvian presence in [*Housekeeping*] [. . .]" (140). Hedrick adds, however:

> What makes *Housekeeping* extraordinary is not its use of Transcendental texts, but its literalization of an attitude toward the house that we accept as masculine and philosophical, but not as feminine and domestic: Women's lives are not supposed to be stripped; they do not engage in man's "morning work," the dusting of the "mind's furniture"; they do not burn down their houses in order to cultivate a "taste for the beautiful." (140)

Robinson makes that feminist point in good humor and without stridency. In fact, one of the novel's funniest passages comes after Ruth has told us that the curtain on Lucille's side of the table had been half consumed by fire from the candles of a birthday cake set too close to it: "Sylvie had beaten out the flames with a back issue of *Good Housekeeping*, but she had never replaced the curtain"

(101). Like the nineteenth-century American authors she emulates, Robinson can be very funny at times, even in a work that is essentially serious and sometimes heartbreaking.

Sylvie as a housekeeping anti-heroine does not amuse Lucille, however. Toward the end of chapter six, we learn that Lucille now has "a familiar" (as Ruth puts it), a girl named Rosette Browne, "whom she feared and admired, and through whose eyes she continually imagined she saw" (103). Lucille has obviously grown apart from Ruth and Sylvie. How did this happen? Marcia Aldrich explains:

> Unlike Ruth, Lucille's identity develops as a result of her recognition of difference, specifically the way Sylvie differs from other girls' mothers, most importantly Rosette Browne's mother, who embroidered dish towels for Rosette's hope chest and took her to Spokane for ballet lessons. [. . .] Lucille defines herself by excluding Sylvie, and eventually her sister, and functions within the given structure of social and sexual roles and relations. Lucille looked "the way one was supposed to look" (121). For Lucille socialization is intimately bound up with an awareness and acceptance of distinct gender roles. (134)

While Lucille distances herself from Sylvie and her sister, Ruth has "feared and suspected that Sylvie and I were of a kind [. . .]" (106). But chapter six ends quietly with Sylvie making pancakes and with the girls attempting to list all the nations of the world.

Chapter seven marks the break between Ruth and Lucille. Significantly, it begins with a quarrel between the sisters about what their mother had been like: "Lucille's mother was orderly, vigorous, and sensible [. . .]," whereas Ruth's "mother presided over a life so strictly simple and circumscribed that it could not have made any significant demands on her attention" (109). Ruth adds an even more telling comment about her mother: "she was the abandoner, and not the one abandoned" (109). Here Ruth states explicitly what the novel has been pointing to all along, namely that, as Christine Caver puts it, "this narrative is deeply rooted in the trauma of abandonment [. . .]" (113). Since such trauma usually renders its victims speechless, we encounter in *Housekeeping* the challenging narrative paradox of a traumatized narrator whose lyrical descriptions rise to the highest levels of eloquence. Caver explains that "Ruth resolves this paradox—the eloquent representation of speechlessness—through a dual-voiced narrative: she *writes* her family history by recording sophisticated and lyrical interior monologues yet is barely able to speak to those around her" (116). What Ruth *says* to others and what she *writes* to us in chapter seven certainly illustrate well Caver's assertion.

Chapter seven continues with Ruth's account of a frightening night that she and Lucille spend beside the lake, during which Ruth grows dreamily distant from her sister. Their trip to the lake begins ominously with the disappearance of their old dog, Crip; but the rest of the day goes by in catching fish and cooking and eating them—in scenes reminiscent of some of the happier adventures of Tom Sawyer and Huckleberry Finn. The girls even find and eat some ripe huckleberries. When the sun goes down and the evening darkens almost before they realize it, they must stay where they are or risk falling into the dark lake because they cannot see to walk safely along the shore. They build a shelter on the beach—"our hut"—but they find it hard to sleep because of wild noises, "like sounds in a dream" (115).

Ruth writes that Lucille would say Ruth fell asleep, but, Ruth adds, in one of her many meditations, "[. . .] I did not. I simply let the darkness in the sky become coextensive with the darkness in my skull and bowels and bones. Everything that falls upon the eye is apparition, a sheet dropped over the world's true workings. The nerves and the brain are tricked, and one is left with dreams [. . .]" (116). Ruth's growing inability to distinguish the dream state from waking reality becomes even more pronounced in chapter eight. Here in chapter seven, the night experience culminates for Ruth in a starkly suicidal thought:

> Darkness is the only solvent. While it was dark, despite Lucille's pacing and whistling, and despite what must have been dreams (since even Sylvie came to haunt me), it seemed to me that there need not be relic, remnant, margin, residue, memento, bequest, memory, thought, track, or trace, if only the darkness could be perfect and permanent. (116)

When the girls begin their return to Fingerbone in the dim early morning light, Ruth almost encounters that perfect darkness. She falls into the lake, and Lucille saves her by pulling her out by her hair. Ruth tells us nothing about her feelings at that time, as if the terror was so great that even writing fails her as a means of communication at this point. By now the reader can recognize, however, that "[t]he lake," as Caver puts it, "as the burial site of both her grandfather and her mother, serves as both metaphor and literal embodiment, as both the emotional and physical site of trauma" (119).

After the girls reach the house and Sylvie seats them in front of the warm stove, wraps them in quilts, and gives them each a cup of "Brimstone tea" (boiling water, condensed milk, and sugar), Ruth falls asleep and dreams that she has died: "So this is all death is, I thought" (118). Sylvie compounds the confusion of dream state with death when she says, after Ruth wakes up, "Sleep is best when you're *really* tired [. . .]. You don't just sleep. You die" (119).

When Ruth wakes, she finds Lucille dressing up to go downtown and buy some hair-setting gel at the drugstore. Lucille asks Ruth to go with her and adds that she dreamed Sylvie was trying to smother her. When they reach the drugstore, they sip Cokes and talk with some older girls. Feeling socially ill at ease, Ruth prepares to leave and tells Lucille: "I just want to go home" (123). Lucille responds by hissing, "That's *Sylvie's* house now" (123). Ruth leaves for home anyway: "For it seemed to me," she writes, "that nothing I had lost, or might lose, could be found there [in the "other world," the conformist community that Lucille is trying to enter], or, to put it another way, it seemed that something I had lost might be found in Sylvie's house" (123-24).

Because the girls have a fight, Lucille ceases trying to persuade Ruth to join her in escaping Sylvie's influence. The girls fight when Lucille attempts to make a dress but Ruth doesn't give her wholehearted support. During the fight, Lucille yells at Ruth: "All you ever do is just stand around like some stupid zombie!" (127). This verbal attack fails to win Ruth's support, but it does reinforce her sense of herself as irredeemably an outcast. She tells us that "[. . .] I had never made a friend in my life" (130). After the fight, Lucille attempts to make the dress all by herself, and her failed attempts to follow the pattern and its directions contrast with Sylvie's simultaneous, undirected, but successful efforts to collect cans.

One evening the girls see Sylvie brushing her hair in exactly the way their mother had brushed her hair the night before her suicide. The coincidence makes Ruth think: "Appearance paints itself on bright and sliding surfaces, for example, memory and dream" (131)—a statement that is not only a further indication that Ruth has trouble telling the difference between dreams and reality but also more evidence of her philosophical bent. Lucille's response to the sight of Sylvie combing her hair the way their mother did hers is to say that she can't wait until she's old enough to leave Fingerbone.

The last part of chapter seven consists of Lucille's three-part campaign to fashion a new life for herself: 1) self-improvement to prepare for a return to school; 2) assimilation into the community of Fingerbone; and 3) rejection of Sylvie and abandonment of Ruth. The girls' return to school includes a scene with the smug and pompous principal, Mr. French—a scene reminiscent of satirical school scenes in Mark Twain's boy books and in the "Trout Fishing in America Terrorists" chapter of Richard Brautigan's *Trout Fishing in America* (1967). Both Lucille and Ruth do manage to satisfy Mr. French's demands for their improved attendance and achievement, Lucille because she wants to do well in school in order to escape Sylvie and, ultimately, Fingerbone; Ruth because she finds doing homework in a classroom, even for the hard classes such as Latin, preferable to being near her peers outside the classroom. At this point, as Christine Caver puts it, "*Housekeeping* endorses neither Fingerbone's socially, spiritually, and intellectually narrow community nor Ruthie's and Lucille's equally unsatisfactory responses to it" (113).

Besides doing well in school, Lucille also starts joining classmates in extracurricular activities. One night in late October, she goes to a dance, and when she returns, she finds on her side of the bed she shares with Ruth that Sylvie is lying there in a kind of trance. Lucille walks out of the room, out of the house, and down the streets of Fingerbone until she arrives at the house of Miss Royce, her Home Economics teacher. Ruth writes that "the two of them talked the night about Lucille's troubles at home" (140). Miss Royce gives Lucille her spare room and, in effect, adopts her. As Ruth puts it, "[. . .] I had no sister after that night" (140). Next morning, Miss Royce comes, has a long talk with Sylvie, and carries away Lucille's schoolbooks and diary. To console Ruth, Sylvie invites her to skip school the next day and join her in a trip on the lake. Ruth agrees to go, and chapter seven ends with the sisters' lives moving noticeably apart.

Chapter eight, preoccupied with metaphors of birth, begins the third section of the novel with a wake-up. Sylvie rouses Ruth from sleep at five a.m. so that they can get an early start to visit the ruins of an old cabin by the lake. More animated in this scene than at any time earlier in the narrative, Sylvie nevertheless has a hard time getting Ruth enthused about going anywhere in the cold late-October morning. As they walk to the lake shore, Ruth thinks: "We are the same. She could as well be my mother. I crouched and slept in her very shape like an unborn child" (145). And after they jump in a boat "borrowed" from an irate owner who yells and throws stones at them from the shore, they have to change positions in the boat so that Sylvie can row. Ruth crawls "under [Sylvie's] body and between her legs" (146), a description that brings to mind the process of a birth. Siân Mile argues, however, that "Sylvie may be the 'mother' of baby Ruth, who 'crawls under her body and out between her legs,' but she does not mother her—she regards Ruth 'without strong emotion' and does not 'wish to remember' her. [. . .] It is 'more than' motherhood that will define the female subject for Robinson" (131).

But Sylvie *does* mother Ruth, not only before the scene in the boat but also not long after it when, after leaving Ruth all day at the ruined house, she returns and holds her distraught niece in a comforting embrace. If Mile is looking at Sylvie as the focus of our attention in these scenes, then it is understandable that Mile sees nothing definitive in them. As Rosowski argues, however, "In *Housekeeping*, Sylvie functions as the private inner self, the alternative to the conforming public self represented by Lucille—not so much a character as a form of self-address by which the dramatic action of Ruth's memory unfolds" (178). I agree with Rosowski; and I also share her view that Robinson uses the birth metaphor "to conceive of birth as a way of knowing [. . .]" (185). The character who gains knowledge from the metaphorical birth is Ruth, not Sylvie.

As Sylvie rows on up the lake, she tells Ruth that she once tried to lure out one of the children that she was sure were near the ruined cabin so that she could see it. But she says she only wanted to see the child, not keep it, and she asks: "What would I do with another child?" (148). Then dawn breaks, reminding Ruth of her grandfather's paintings; and when she thinks of him, she imagines Sylvie and herself being drawn down into the lake in a vortex and passing her grandfather in his Pullman berth (150). Later in chapter eight, when Ruth and Sylvie are back on the lake returning from the ruined house, Ruth again imagines being pulled to the bottom of the lake and becoming so filled with water that there "would come parturition in some form [. . .]" (162). Then Ruth writes: "The only true birth would be a final one, which would free us from watery darkness and the thought of watery darkness, but could such a birth be imagined?" (162). As Caver views this passage,

> Ruth's obsession with the only "true birth"—death—captures the paradox of her life: she cannot imagine ever being free from the "watery darkness" that filters her perception of the world and thus is drawn to the death that would literalize her perception. The escape from rigid borders into liquidity is in no way an unproblematic liberation in this novel. (128)

Keep in mind, however, that when Ruth has these obsessive speculations about death, she is in the midst of an unsettling experience.

For in the visit to the ruined cabin, Ruth has had to confront loneliness, abandonment, and the strength of her own desire. At the cabin with Sylvie, noticing the beautiful effect of the sunlight on the frost, Ruth makes another of her speculative analogies. The passage is so striking that it is often quoted in full by reviewers and critics, and it follows here in full, as well:

> Imagine a Carthage sown with salt, and all the sowers gone, and the seeds lain however long in the earth, till there rose finally in vegetable profusion leaves and trees of rime and brine. What flowering would there be in such a garden? Light would force each salt calyx to open in prisms, and to fruit heavily with bright globes of water—peaches and grapes are little more than that, and where the world was salt there would be greater need of slaking. For need can blossom into all the compensations it requires. To crave and to have are as like as a thing and its shadow. For when does a berry break upon the tongue as sweetly as when one longs to taste it, and when is the taste refracted into so many hues and savors of ripeness and earth, and when do our senses know anything so utterly as when we lack it? And here again is a foreshadowing—the world will be made whole. For to wish for a hand on one's hair is all but to feel it. So whatever we may lose, very craving gives it back to us again. Though we dream and hardly know it, longing, like an angel, fosters us, smooths our hair, and brings us wild strawberries. (152-53)

Of the allusion to Carthage in that extraordinary passage, Gary Williams has written at some length. He points out that Rome's destruction of Carthage in 146 BCE meant "the dominance of Greco-Roman values in Western culture" (71). He also notes that because the Roman victors wrote the histories of the Punic Wars, our knowledge of Carthage consists largely of the Romans' very unflattering accounts of their conquered enemy. Some evidence exists, however, that shows Carthaginians were more attuned to nature than were their Roman foes, and Williams says the Carthaginian goddess Tanit is associated "with the moon and thus with darkness [. . .]" (74). Sylvie prefers darkness, whereas Lucille chooses light; and the Latin roots of her name, *lucere* (to shine) and *lux* (light), "may also tie her to Lucifer, a name for Venus in her manifestation as the morning star" (74).

Moreover, Williams sees the birth imagery in chapter eight differently from the way Caver views it. He says that "[. . .] Sylvie is the midwife, is Tanit [. . .], assisting Ruth in her birth into a new perception" (75). Williams concludes:

> The perceptual environment that Ruth speaks from bears the same relation to the dominant value system in American culture that Carthage bore to Rome: it is a mystical, dreaming, moon-and-water, death-and-flux-accepting state of mind, utterly at odds with that expressed in Ruth's vision of those who refurbish the house she and Sylvie have relinquished [. . .]. (76)

What Williams says makes good sense, since Americans, from the time of the early republic to our own day, have seen similarities between the ancient Romans and our own civilization.

One parallel between ancient Rome and America that Williams and other critics of *Housekeeping* do not mention is the similarity between the Romans' conquest of the Carthaginians and the European Americans' subjugation of American Indians. Although Ruth mentions Indians only a few times in passing, readers will either know or guess that the lake near Fingerbone not only holds the remains of Edmund Foster, his fellow riders on the Fireball, and his daughter Helen Stone but also may be the final resting place of the corpses of countless Indians who must have perished in the vicinity of the lake during the hundreds of years Indian peoples lived in the area. Like the Carthaginians, the American

Indians were misunderstood and mischaracterized by those who conquered them. Regardless of what the Indians might have done if they had ever built large cities, before the arrival of Columbus, the first peoples of North America lived in greater harmony with the natural world than have their European American conquerors.

More significantly, even many of the Indians who lived in immovable dwellings were at least semi-nomadic. Like the transients in *Housekeeping*, the Indians felt at home in nature and periodically moved from place to place. As Roy Harvey Pearce, Leslie Fiedler, Richard Slotkin, William Scheick, and other scholars have explained, in the Euro-American mind the Indian functions as the Other, as a being whose differences from us—at least as we perceive those putative differences—help us to define our own identity. Like the Romans, Americans for centuries often saw the people they subjugated in negative terms, a myopia that made it all the easier to see themselves as God's chosen people, superior and deserving of victory and its spoils. Pushed onto reservations, Indians had been moved out of sight but not out of mind. Hoboes, tramps, and other transients eventually appeared on the American scene to play the role of stand-ins for the Indians. The good conformists of Fingerbone shudder at Sylvie's lifestyle because it marks her so clearly as a renegade who has gone over to an Indian style of life.

George Toles takes a different view of the otherness in *Housekeeping*. He says that Robinson personifies the Others in the novel not as Indians but rather "as the spirits of wild, orphan children, permanently in the cold" (144). Toles offers his observation in a detailed essay about the significance of the Carthage passage in *Housekeeping*. He says that Ruth's language, used to express her version of Dickinson's idea of "sumptuous Destitution," is scriptural.

> The silence attending the solemn assurance that need will itself restore what is gone is like the silence attending Jesus's parables: "He who has ears to hear, let him hear." Whatever analogies are drawn from experience to reveal the meaning of Jesus's parables, no appeal to experience is sufficient to nullify or refute that meaning. In the language of Mikhail Bakhtin, scriptural truth is termed "absolute utterance," the kind of word that admits no authorship. Absolute utterance "can only be cited, and recited. When spoken, it belongs to no one; when written, it is Scripture." (148)

According to Toles, Ruth's meditation is, like Jesus' parables, a kind of "absolute utterance," carrying for Ruth the truth of scripture.

Whether the Carthage passage is scripture or a prose poem or both, it is, as Rosowski writes, a "meditative exercise," in which "understanding produces emotions and acts of will in an extension of the self to other human beings, nature, and the supernatural. Without Lucille (her public self) and with Sylvie (the dramatic form of her self-address) Ruth achieves the heightened receptivity of a solitary self" (184). Ruth's receptivity opens her to profound insights, but however much these insights satisfy Ruth's need for understanding, they offer little in the way of immediate solace, at least judging from what happens by the ruined house.

Although nothing in the passage itself indicates whether Ruth imagined "a Carthage sown with salt" at the time of her trip with Sylvie or thought of it later, the text of the novel provides evidence that she probably fell into the reverie at the time of the visit, because the first line after the Carthage passage reads: "Sylvie was gone" (153). If Ruth had not been absorbed in imagining a Carthage sown in salt, she probably would have noticed Sylvie's departure. Some of the remaining speculative analogies in chapter eight do include wording that shows Ruth thought of them at the time of the trip with Sylvie. This succession of powerful reveries probably arises from the intense psychological and emotional turmoil stirred up by Lucille's departure and by the trip with Sylvie. Most of these hypothetical analogies include hardship, discomfort, loneliness, and death—and sometimes, too, the compensations life gives.

With Sylvie gone, Ruth walks down to the lakeshore and feels in the adjoining woods the presence of the children Sylvie had said she would find. When neither the children nor Sylvie appears, Ruth walks back to the ruins of the old house. Her exploration in the ruins leads her to a reverie about what might have happened to its occupants. She associates the loneliness of the dispersed occupants with the loneliness of certain people in bus stations. She concludes: "[O]nce alone, it is impossible to believe that one could ever have been otherwise. Loneliness is an absolute discovery" (157).

Then Ruth begins pulling loose planks out of the cellar hole, but her efforts turn up nothing but more imagining about doomed children and about what would happen if her grandmother's house collapsed "while we were sleeping [. . .]" (159). This last thought brings her to a Thoreauvian conclusion: "It is better to have nothing, for at last even our bones will fall. It is better to have nothing" (159). Ruth's repetitiveness here suggests she is trying to convince herself that such total abnegation really is best.

Alone in the growing cold and the dying of the day, Ruth reaches a moment of resignation in the face of terror: "I thought, Sylvie is nowhere, and sometime it will be dark. I thought, Let them [the ghost children] come unhouse me of this flesh, and pry this house apart" (159). Just as soon as she has resigned herself to being taken by the ghost children, Ruth begins yearning to see her mother. Ruth writes that she knows the lake has taken her mother's body but she still hopes to see her essence, and she says of her mother: "She was a music I no longer heard, that rang in my mind, itself and nothing else, lost to all sense, but not perished, not perished" (160). The repetitiveness this time suggests still-grief-stricken denial rather than certain conviction.

At this crucial moment, Ruth writes, "Sylvie put her hand on my back" (160). Once Sylvie has looked into Ruth's face and, presumably, seen the emotional and psychological distress that is probably displayed there, she opens her coat and takes Ruth into a motherly embrace. Ruth feels simultaneously both anger and gratitude because Sylvie left her for so long but finally returned to rescue her from loneliness. This scene, it seems to me, supports Karen Kaivola's view that "Robinson does not offer a new and politically promising female subjectivity. What she does, instead, is represent how compelling it can be—especially in the context of significant loss and perhaps especially for women—to try to overrun boundaries between self and other, to merge, to be absorbed" (688).

When Ruth recounts their getting back in the boat and traveling down the lake toward Fingerbone, she contrasts Sylvie's sense of time with her own. "Sylvie had no sense of time," Ruth writes, whereas, "I hated waiting"; and "my life seemed composed entirely of expectation" (165-66). Then Ruth reveals how deeply troubled Sylvie remains as a result of her father's and sister's deaths. In spite of the lateness and the cold and their hunger, Sylvie rows the boat up next to the railroad bridge and waits for the next train. When it has passed, Ruth writes, Sylvie "folded her arms on her knees and buried her face, and she swayed and swayed and swayed [. . .]" (167). Sylvie's obsessive grieving shows that she needs Ruth as much as, if not more than, Ruth needs her.

After they reach the shore and beach the boat, they wait for an eastbound train, and when one arrives and slows for the bridge, they clamber into a boxcar, in a corner of which an old Indian woman sits. Morning has arrived, and as they look out over the lake, Ruth imagines what it was like "at the apex of the Flood [. . .] when Noah's wife must have opened the shutters upon a morning designed to reflect an enormous good nature" (172). But Ruth's reverie follows the usual path of her speculation, and she further imagines that when old, Noah's wife might have "found somewhere a remnant of the Deluge [. . .]" and walked into it. Ruth seems to feel that such a death would be fitting, since Noah's wife "was a nameless woman and so at home among all those who were never found and never missed, who were uncommemorated, whose deaths were not remarked, nor their begettings" (172). Martha Ravits points out that Noah's unnamed wife is one of a number of biblical women (Ruth, Naomi, and Lot's wife are the others) to whom Robinson's Ruth alludes. "By highlighting aspects of these female figures," Ravits says, "Robinson makes these symbolic women of woe cast shadows upon the modern page in an act of literary revisionism [. . .]" (657).

In addition to her allusions to biblical women, Robinson includes another striking act of literary revisionism. Rosowski summarizes it as follows:

> Whereas the biblical Genesis establishes a forward movement of creation *ex nihilo* driven by acts that divide and separate (God makes heaven and earth out of nothing, then separates darkness from light, matter from air, woman from man), *Housekeeping* reverses the movement. It returns light to darkness, form to void, and the many to the one when Ruth pursues the memory of a lake and its associations with birth until she reaches the void and discovers the loneliness from which arises the need of analogue. (179)

Housekeeping, Rosowski further suggests, can be compared with the poetry of Wallace Stevens, in that Robinson's novel is Ruth's "record of a mind finding what will suffice" (179).

When Ruth and Sylvie finally reach home, Sylvie makes a fire in the stove and goes off to her room to lie down. Ruth writes that while sitting by the stove, "I was almost asleep, or I was asleep, when Lucille came into the kitchen and sat down in Sylvie's chair" (174). Ruth's uncertainty makes it impossible to know not only whether Lucille actually appeared but also whether Ruth was dreaming or just deep in one of her speculative reveries. Whatever the case may be, she also writes that at this point she has a series of dreams: of her and Sylvie drifting in the dark; of trains sliding into the lake as if the bridge were a chute; and of the bridge as the frame of a charred house whose lost children she and Sylvie search for unsuccessfully.

Here is her description of the last of those dreams: "I dreamed that Sylvie was teaching me to walk under water. To move so slowly needed patience and grace, but she pulled me after her in the slowest waltz, and our clothes flew like the robes of painted angels" (175). This dream dance has similarities with the dance described in Theodore Roethke's well-known poem "My Papa's Waltz," in that both "waltzes" include an older family member moving a child through the movements of a dance in a way that mixes affection with fear. Thomas Gardner says that Ruth's dream of Sylvie's waltz "is in fact a description of the slow patient style of Ruth's own narration—her voice, in its speculative *says* and *imagines*, a slow waltz through a vast world of fragments, none of which offers a permanent home [. . .]" (28). The dream dance also reminds us of the time during the flooding from the lake when, Ruth writes, "Sylvie took me by the hands and pulled me after her through six grand waltz steps" (64). That waltz had led to one of Ruth's earlier speculative reveries: "I imagined her [Sylvie] seizing my hands and pulling me after her in a wild waltz down the hall, through the kitchen, through the orchard, the night moonless and I in my nightgown, almost asleep" (68). Chapter eight, then, ends with Ruth's feeling that Sylvie is teaching her a way to respond to the grief and loneliness that pervade their lives.

Chapter nine tells about Fingerbone's response to the ride that Sylvie took Ruth on in the railroad boxcar, proof to the citizens of Fingerbone that "Sylvie was an unredeemed transient, and she was making a transient of me" (177). Fingerbonians find transients unsettling, Ruth writes, even "terrifying as ghosts are because they were not very different from us" (178). To rescue Ruth, Fingerbone's sheriff is sent to assess Sylvie's housekeeping and to serve as a warning to her that she must abandon her transient ways if she hopes to keep Ruth. Hard on the sheriff's heels are the good Christian ladies of Fingerbone, who are, of course, appalled by Sylvie's accumulations of tin cans and old newspapers and magazines, not to mention the body parts of sparrows left around the house by the thirteen or fourteen cats now part of the household. To get us to understand how the ladies find Sylvie's self-assurance the most threatening, Ruth asks us to imagine how Noah's neighbors would have felt if they had seen him knocking his house apart to build the ark. Noah would have told them that "[a] house should have a compass and a keel" (184); and hearing that, they would have "found their own houses wanting in ways they could not understand" (184). Talking with Sylvie makes the ladies of Fingerbone feel their lives are wanting in ways they cannot understand.

Yet Sylvie eventually responds to the visits of the sheriff and the ladies by attempting to make herself and Ruth and their house more normal; and Ruth does her best to help achieve normalcy. Sylvie undertakes a conventional housecleaning and begins cooking conventional meals. For her part, Ruth puts on her nicest clothes and goes back to school. More importantly, Ruth starts to realize just how much Sylvie cares for her: "I was surprised, in fact, that she would go to such lengths for my sake" (189). We see in Sylvie's replies to the ladies' well-meaning questions just how deeply disturbed she still is from the trauma of the deaths of her father and sister. At the end of an anecdote that Sylvie tells about a woman who was "probably crazy," an anecdote told to illustrate her assertion that "[t]hat's how it is with family [. . .]. You feel them the most when they're gone," Sylvie incoherently blurts out, "Helen and Papa were never close" (185). Because Ruth knows that the ladies can tell just how disturbed Sylvie is, she is not surprised when the sheriff arrives again to tell Sylvie that there will be a hearing about taking Ruth from her. Sylvie says to the sheriff, "It's a terrible thing to break up a family"; but Ruth writes: "I knew we were doomed" (190). And on that note, chapter nine ends.

Surprisingly, chapter ten does not begin with a continued account of the confrontation between Sylvie and the sheriff. Instead, it starts with Ruth's interpretations of, and meditations upon, some biblical stories of familial loss: "Cain murdered Abel, and blood cried out from the earth; [. . .] and Rachel mourned for her children; and King David for Absalom. The force behind the movement of time is a mourning that will not be comforted" (192). As Ruth sees it, by sending the Flood, God purged the "wicked sadness" left by Cain's murder of Abel. And Ruth links the catastrophe of the biblical Deluge to what happened to her grandfather and mother:

> I cannot taste a cup of water but I recall that the eye of the lake is my grandfather's, and that the lake's heavy, blind, encumbering waters composed my mother's limbs and weighed her garments and stopped her breath and stopped her sight. (193-94)

For Ruth, however, the lake's power could cause sorrow but not the obliteration of memory: "There is remembrance, and communion, altogether human and unhallowed. For families will not be broken" (194).

Then, after writing that "[m]emory is loss, and loss pulls us after it" (194), Ruth offers an interpretation of the life of Jesus. In a version of Emily Dickinson's idea of "sumptuous Destitution," Ruth even says that the resurrection resulted from the longing of Jesus's friends to have him back with them. So, she says, do human beings have "the hope that memory will fulfill itself, and become flesh [. . .]" (195). We find next that Ruth's interpretations of biblical stories are meant to explain why, as she puts it, "Sylvie did not want to lose me" (195). Sylvie wants Ruth to be with her so that Ruth will not, by her absence, fill all Sylvie's waking thoughts and cause pained longing for her return.

Then Ruth offers us one of her most poignant speculative analogies. She asks us to "[i]magine that [her] mother had come back that evening [. . .]" (195). Ruth intersperses passages of her hypothesis of what it would have been like if her mother had *not* killed herself with a more detailed description of the trip from Seattle to Fingerbone on the day when her mother drove into the lake. Ruth even imagines how she and Lucille would have felt and acted over a lifetime if their mother had returned and lived into old age. Because of her mother's apparent calm, Ruth believes that she and Lucille "would have known nothing of the nature and reach of her sorrow if she had come back" (198). Learning of her mother's sorrow has its consequences, too. Ruth writes: "Even the illusion of perimeters fails when families are separated" (198).

At this point in chapter ten, Ruth returns to her narrative about Sylvie's desperate efforts not to lose the niece remaining with her. "Sylvie realized that her first scheme to keep us together had failed" (198), Ruth writes. "Still, [Sylvie] persisted in her housekeeping" (199). Her persistence consists of burning all the old newspapers and magazines on a bonfire. Seeing all those pages of print go up in flames makes Ruth realize "that things were held in place, are held in place, by a web of words" (200). Sylvie even burns a book, *Not as a Stranger*, and tells Ruth, "That isn't the sort of thing you should be reading [. . .]" (200). With another touch of humor, Ruth tells us: "This was intended to impress the judicial gentlemen in the orchard, so I did not tell her it was a library book" (200-01).

Burning the library book underscores Sylvie's failure to adopt accepted modes of behavior, since she uses unconventional and, to many, repugnant means (burning a book) in order to convince her fellow townspeople that she is normal and trustworthy. Moreover, the reference to Morton Thompson's *Not as a Stranger* (published by Scribner in 1954 and the number-one bestseller of that year) not only helps us to date the events of the novel (the bonfire scene obviously cannot take place before 1954) but also reminds us of the prevailing moral, social, and aesthetic standards in small towns of the mid to late 1950s. *Not as a Stranger* tells the story of Lucas Marsh, who struggles from boyhood to become a doctor and eventually succeeds in doing so. What would probably have made Sylvie think that Thompson's novel was not the sort of book an adolescent girl should read were the scenes of sexual intimacy (scenes which, by today's standards, are not very graphic).

After all the magazines, newspapers, and *Not as a Stranger* have burned, Sylvie tells Ruth to go in while she puts dirt on the ashes. But instead of going into the house, Ruth hides in the dark and, when Sylvie comes to find her, runs into the orchard. From where Ruth stands among the darkened trees, this is what she sees: "The house stood out beyond the orchard with every one of its windows lighted. It looked large, and foreign, and contained, like a moored ship—a fantastic thing to find in a garden" (203). The comparison of the house to a ship brings to mind Ruth's earlier description of Noah pulling apart the boards of his house to build an ark. Ruth writes that she "could not imagine going into it [the lighted house that now looks to her like a ship]" (203). Instead of going in, she begins imagining a story: "Once there was a young girl strolling at night in an orchard" (203).

As the story proceeds, Ruth reveals that the girl is some sort of wraith, but the "gross light" from the windows of a house transforms her "into a mortal child" (204). Standing "at the bright window," the child discovers that all has gone, including her mother, grandmother, and aunts. Then Ruth says: "Like Noah's wife on the tenth or fifteenth night of rain, she would stand in the window and realize that the world was really lost. And those outside would scarcely know her, so sadly was she changed" (204). Brief though it is, Ruth's story reminds one of the tales of Nathaniel Hawthorne, with their powerful symbolism. Since Ruth shows that she can emulate authors such as Dickinson and Hawthorne, we cannot reasonably conclude that she follows Sylvie into a life of transience because she lacks the intelligence and imagination to choose another course of action. Ruth's point in telling the story, however, is to illustrate what must be done to survive great hardship: namely, "if you do not resist the cold, but simply relax and accept it, you no longer feel the cold as discomfort" (204). Along with this realization, Ruth writes, "[. . .] I could feel that I was breaking the tethers of need, one by one" (204).

Ruth has become, in other words, a latter-day Diogenes, free because she no longer needs anything. At this point, the sheriff arrives to find out why all the lights are on in a house that has been conspicuously dark for months. When he orders Sylvie to let him see Ruth so that he can be sure the girl is all right, Ruth gives up her game of hide-and-seek, steps out of the dark, and stands beside Sylvie. Chapter ten ends with the sheriff ordering Ruth to go to bed and to be in school the next day and telling Sylvie to be there when he comes back the next day.

Chapter eleven, the final chapter, brings *Housekeeping* to an ending saturated with ambiguity. It begins with Sylvie and Ruth's decision not only to leave Fingerbone before the sheriff returns the next day, but also to set fire to the house, since they cannot bear to leave it behind, "its relics to be pawed" by "the needy and the parsimonious of Fingerbone" (209). The aunt and her niece believe that to stay would mean separation, and since they will not part, Ruth writes: "Now truly we were cast out to wander, and there was an end to housekeeping" (209). Farcically, however, the house "would *not* burn" (208). Hearing the approach of the train on which they plan to depart, Sylvie takes the burning broom she has used to light the pantry curtain and the rug's fringe and tosses it at the woodpile. Then she and Ruth run out the door, through the orchard, to the edge of the field they need to pass through to reach the train. But they are too late: the train passes in front of them before they can get to it.

Since they can see neither smoke nor flames in the direction of the house, Sylvie concludes that the fire must not have been enough to burn down the house. She thinks the townspeople will soon discover that she and Ruth are not there and will begin to search for them. Not wanting to be found and arrested, Sylvie and Ruth decide to walk across the railroad bridge, since Sylvie is sure that no one will think they would attempt such a foolhardy feat. The implication is that everyone in Fingerbone knows that trying to cross the bridge in the dark is so risky that it would be tantamount to playing Russian roulette. Ruth writes that, at first, the crossing "was easy enough" (211), but then a watery wind begins to blow, and "[i]t was so dark there might have been no Sylvie ahead of me, and the bridge might have created itself under my foot as I walked, and vanished again behind me" (212).

The creaking of the bridge as the lake current pulls at it makes Ruth "think of a park where my mother used to take Lucille and me" (212). Remembering the details of one visit in particular, Ruth realizes that she and Lucille never knew why their mother was happy or sad. They could tell only that "[i]t was as if she righted herself continually against some current that never ceased to pull. She swayed continuously, like a thing in water, and it was graceful, a slow dance, a sad and heady dance" (213). The swaying reminds us of Sylvie's earlier motion when she and Ruth watched from the boat as a train crossed the bridge; Helen's dance resembles the one that Ruth dreams Sylvie teaches her; and the water they all dance in is most likely the grief they feel at the abandonment caused by their parents' deaths.

At this point, there is a section break in chapter eleven. This particular section break creates an especially wide gap in the narrative, since the reader expects Ruth to finish describing the crossing of the bridge. Instead of doing so, Ruth begins the new section (on page 213) by telling us that Sylvie has pinned to the underside of her right lapel a newspaper clipping that reports her and Ruth's presumed deaths in the attempted crossing. Of course, a reader will probably assume that since Ruth is telling the story, she must have survived the crossing; but the gap in the text introduces an element of uncertainty (Why wouldn't Ruth finish describing the crossing?); and for some readers the uncertainty leads to the possibility that we are meant to think of Ruth as telling us her story after she has died. If that seems too improbable, recall the many proleptic narratives in Dickinson's poems and the effects created by having speakers who are already dead.

Whether she's dead or alive when she writes, Ruth tells us, "It happened many years ago, now, and the worst of it is that in all those years we have never contacted Lucille" (213). Sylvie and Ruth have become drifters (either imaginary or real, depending on whether you think they survived the crossing), although occasionally Ruth will take a job as a waitress or a clerk until customers and fellow workers sense something odd about her, and then she and Sylvie resort to drifting again.

"When did I become so unlike other people?" Ruth asks. She says it was either when she followed Sylvie across the bridge or when her mother left her waiting or when she was conceived. Ruth's meditation on her conception matches the eloquence of a Shakespearean or Melvillean monologue:

> Of my conception I know only what you know of yours. It occurred in darkness and I was unconsenting. I (and that slenderest word is too gross for the rare thing I was then) walked forever through reachless oblivion, in the mood of one smelling night-blooming flowers, and suddenly—My ravishers left their traces in me, male and female, and over the months I rounded, grew heavy, until the scandal could no longer be concealed and oblivion expelled me. But this I have in common with all my kind. By some bleak alchemy what had been mere unbeing becomes death when life is mingled with it. So they seal the door against our returning. (214-15)

In this passage worthy of Hamlet and Ishmael, Ruth rails with a remarkable eloquence against the Power that has brought her into a world of such sorrow.

Nevertheless, Ruth concludes that "it was the crossing of the bridge that changed me finally" (215). She says that she stumbled and fell twice. Are we to believe that she and Sylvie survived such a crossing? Or is it a ghost who tells the story of *Housekeeping*, a spirit who, even when she took human form, "never distinguished readily between thinking and dreaming" (215)? Ruth tries to allay our doubts at this point by saying, "I will try to tell you the plain truth" (216). And then she says that she and Sylvie made it across the bridge, hopped a train, and have drifted around the west, mostly the northwest, ever since. Ruth, still wanting to find Lucille, writes: "Someday when I am feeling presentable I will go into Fingerbone and make inquiries. I must do it soon, for such days are rare now" (217). Implicit in her statement is the possibility that she is sinking, at last, into clinical depression so deep that she will not return from it.

After another section break, Ruth writes: "All this is fact. Fact explains nothing. On the contrary, it is fact that requires explanation" (217). But instead of explaining, Ruth offers two more speculative reveries. In the first, she says that—in her mind—Lucille has lived in the family house all the years since she and Sylvie left: "Since we are dead [officially, at least], the house would be hers now" (217-18). Ruth asks: "What if I should walk to the house one night and find Lucille there?" (217). But Ruth's imagining does not extend to picturing a scene of reunion. She imagines, instead, that if Lucille were living in the house, she would attribute otherwise inexplicable matters such as opened doors and tipped vases to Ruth and Sylvie's doing. Then, "She would sigh and think, 'They never change'" (218).

Ruth's second speculative reverie, the one that ends the novel, imagines "[. . .] Lucille in Boston, at a table in a restaurant, waiting for a friend" (218). Ruth pictures her sister as being "tastefully dressed" (218). Then the reverie shifts focus to emphasize that Ruth and Sylvie "are nowhere in Boston" (218) and will never be there. Nevertheless, Ruth writes, Lucille's "thoughts are thronged by our absence [. . .] and she does not watch, does not listen, does not wait, does not hope, and always for me and Sylvie" (219). That paradoxical observation that Lucille cannot *not* wait for Sylvie and Ruth without always having them in mind is similar to the view that an atheist must have in mind the god that he says he does not believe in. With that thought, *Housekeeping* ends.

The ending, however, answers explicitly none of the questions that it raises. Like some other great novels—*The Scarlet Letter*, for example—*Housekeeping* ends in ambiguity that forces each reader to interpret the narrative in whatever way seems best. Some readers will agree with Christine Caver that Sylvie and Ruth may not have survived the bridge crossing and are, in any case, victims of the trauma of abandonment. As Caver puts it, "[T]he metaphor employed to portray her [Ruth's] escape with Sylvie from Fingerbone [. . .] [is] a metaphor long associated with the crossing from the world of the living to the world of the dead—a metaphor strongly suggesting that their flight is into social, if not literal, death [. . .]" (131). For readers who agree with Caver or who feel certain that Ruth and Sylvie die in the crossing, Ruth's final two speculative hypotheses accentuate the loss, bereavement, and abandonment that appear throughout the novel. Ruth's proleptic narrative will probably strike such readers as a haunting solution to the authorial problem of how to give voice to those rendered speechless by trauma.

Other critics and readers believe that Sylvie and Ruth survive the crossing. Seen from that perspective, the ending offers two plausible fates for Lucille. Whether in Fingerbone or in Boston, Lucille would probably have led a conventional life in an effort to fit in with the respectable members of either community. It is possible in this interpretation, too, to see Ruth as narrating in the voice of one who is dead, since she is listed as dead in the official records and since she is dead to her sister. In this interpretation, Ruth's proleptic narration accentuates the irony of the difference between what Lucille thinks and what is actually the case.

Of disagreements over the ending, Rosowski says:

> I am amused at speculations that Ruth and Sylvie died in their attempt to cross the bridge [. . .]. The question of their death is quite beside the point in a novel that breaks down divisions of men/women, East/West, culture/nature, and life/death. The pertinent question has to do with language. Do Ruth and Sylvie inhabit our language and thus our consciousness? Is the Ruth of *Housekeeping* free of Robinson,

having become part of the stories now growing inside her readers? Do we recognize ourselves in her and become her ghost children, pulled toward a conception of ourselves? (187)

Rosowski is right about what is the pertinent question, but the novel's ambiguous ending, including the matter of Ruth and Sylvie's death or survival, may be what eventually leads many readers to the insight Rosowski articulates so well.

As I read *Housekeeping*, Ruth and Sylvie do survive the bridge crossing, although they remain victims, as they have been all along. For me, the ending illuminates the nature of Ruth's sacrifice. Like the biblical Ruth, Ruth Stone has left one community and entered another out of love. She knows that Lucille can survive on her own—in fact, Lucille has virtually rejected Ruth in order to gain social acceptance in Fingerbone. Ruth also knows that Sylvie needs her. The evidence shows that Edmund Foster's death has traumatized Sylvie far more than Ruth is affected by her mother's suicide, although Ruth also bears wounds caused by the trauma of abandonment. Sylvie, however, falls into trance-like states, she sways uncontrollably when the train passes overhead, and—in spite of her love for Ruth—she fails at the kind of housekeeping needed to maintain Fingerbone's approval of her guardianship of her nieces. Ruth, on the other hand, does not take naturally to a life of transience. Although she learns to break "the tethers of need," she is naturally averse to the cold—and it's obvious that she loves the life of the mind, not life on the road (204).

That is not to say that she would prefer Lucille's conventional existence to transience with Sylvie. Ruth stays with her aunt because she loves her; and also, as a result of her own trauma at the death of her mother, she understands the forces that have unmoored Sylvie's spirit, making her a restless drifter. Emotionally devastated by the sense of abandonment caused by her father's and sister's deaths, Sylvie lives almost instinctively. But Ruth lives on the road the way Thoreau lived at Walden Pond and the way Dickinson lived in her Amherst bedroom: all three use language and the mind to fashion a life that enriches the soul.

Ruth's paramount reason for choosing to follow Sylvie is love. In that respect, *Housekeeping* is a contemporary Book of Ruth; and Ruth's gift of love ranks with Rose of Sharon's act of love at the end of Steinbeck's *The Grapes of Wrath*. Robinson's latter-day scripture is also a work of western American literature, not only because of its setting but also because it uses that setting to place the human drama in a context of geologic time. Seen in that context, the houses no longer have a fixed, lasting quality but seem evanescent, scarcely more substantial than the cobwebs in their corners. Having been shown as essentially flimsy by that shift in perspective, the houses of Fingerbone undermine any sense that fixed abodes are the "natural" dwellings for human beings. Ruth's reveries and meditations—like the works of Thoreau, Dickinson, Emerson, Poe, Hawthorne, and Melville—remind us that the housekeeping of the soul should have precedence over the housekeeping of any pile of boards and bricks.

America's high culture has always given such a reminder. Popular culture and the mass mind, however, revere the material monuments of America's past as if they were more important than the soul. Hollywood, for example, presents our buildings as icons, material symbols that moviemakers try to invest with more sacrality than the earth itself. But, as Heather Bohannan argues, "Ruth and Sylvie [. . .] experience the sacred as *immanence in* the world rather than *transcendence beyond* it" (75). Small wonder, then, that even a well-intentioned attempt to make a movie version of *Housekeeping* resulted in a film quite different from the novel, in spite of a generally faithful adherence to the storyline. The movie, also titled *Housekeeping*, was directed by Bill Forsyth and released by Columbia in 1987. Sheila Ruzycki O'Brien argues that Forsyth takes Robinson's reshaping of the traditional American western into a New West tale and makes a film that reverts to the Old West tradition.

Like other works of late twentieth-century western American literature that are now regarded as not only regional but also national classics, *Housekeeping* pushes our thinking in the direction of a post-frontier west. The novel shares with Gary Snyder's *Mountains and Rivers Without End* (1996), for example, the recognition that, as Snyder puts it, to "grasp the common-sense truth of impermanence is to realize your physical limitations. [. . .] Then, to grasp the somewhat less common-sense truth of no self is to realize that the boundaries between inside and outside, yourself and the surroundings, is [sic] permeable, and that air and water of this neighborhood, this valley, is [sic] also inextricably part of your being" (qtd. in Smith 46). Ruth Stone's narrative also contains the truths that Snyder mentions. When, in our imaginations, we cross the bridge with Ruth and Sylvie, we go imaginatively from the mindset of the Old West to the more soul-centered vision of the post-frontier west.

Are Ruth and Sylvie feminist heroines, then? In the risks they take for love, these women are, indeed, heroic. They are also victims of the trauma caused by the deaths of their family members; and they remain victims because no one (but the other) recognizes the nature and depth of their suffering. Ruth sacrifices much of her life out of love for Sylvie and without a hint of a modern-day Boaz on the horizon. As Emerson and Dickinson urge us to do, Ruth allows her inner being to shape her life: she follows wherever love takes her. To meet the needs of love, there was, indeed, as Ruth says, "an end to housekeeping" of the old order, the Old West (209). But Robinson's novel invites us to a new order of housekeeping, one that leaves behind the houses of frontier thinking—barriers between Us and Them, between civilization and nature. This new housekeeping cannot sweep sorrow from our lives but it can tend the connections between inner and outer being, making us more attuned to ourselves, to the world, and to everything in it.

Selected Bibliography

Note: Biblical references in the text are taken from the King James Version.

WORKS BY MARILYNNE ROBINSON

The Death of Adam: Essays on Modern Thought. Boston: Houghton, 1998.

"The First and Second Epistles General of Peter." *Incarnation: Contemporary Writers on the New Testament*. Ed. Alfred Corn. New York: Viking, 1990. 305-15.

"Gospels." *Communion: Contemporary Writers Reveal the Bible in Their Lives*. Ed. David Rosenberg. New York: Anchor, 1996. 133-49.

"Hearing Silence: Western Myth Reconsidered." *The True Subject: Writers on Life and Craft*. Ed. Kurt Brown. St. Paul, MN: Graywolf, 1993. 135-51.

Housekeeping. New York: Farrar, 1981; Bantam, 1982.

Mother Country. New York: Farrar, 1989.

"My Western Roots." *Old West—New West: Centennial Essays*. Ed. Barbara Howard Meldrum. Moscow: U of Idaho P, 1993. 165-72.

"A New Look at Shakespeare's *Henry VI, Part II*: Sources, Structure and Meaning." Dissertation. U of Washington, 1977.

BIBLIOGRAPHIES

Durose, Lisa. "Marilynne Robinson: A Bibliography." *ANQ [American Notes and Queries]* 10.1 (Winter 1997): 31-46.

INTERVIEWS WITH MARILYNNE ROBINSON

Bartos, Eileen, Tace Hedrick, Carolyn Jacobson, and Ann E. Voss. "Interviews with Marilynne Robinson." *Iowa Review* 22.1 (Winter 1992): 1-28.

Bonetti, Kay. *An Interview with Marilynne Robinson.* Audiocassette. Columbia, MO: American Audio Prose Library, 1989.

Boyers, Robert. "Talking about American Fiction" [a panel discussion with Marilynne Robinson, Russell Banks, Robert Stone, and David Rieft]. *Salmagundi* 93 (1992): 61-77.

"Hum Inside the Skull: A Symposium." *New York Times Book Review* 13 May 1984: 1, 30.

O'Connell, Nicholas. "Marilynne Robinson." *At the Field's End: Interviews with Twenty Pacific Northwest Writers.* Seattle: Madrona, 1987. 220-30.

Pinsker, Sandford. "Conversation with Marilynne Robinson." *Conversations with Contemporary American Writers.* Amsterdam: Rodopi, 1985. 119-27.

Robinson, Marilynne. *Morning Edition.* National Public Radio. 28 Nov. 1987.

Schaub, Thomas. "An Interview with Marilynne Robinson." *Contemporary Literature* 35.2 (1994): 231-51.

Vorda, Allan. "A Life of Perished Things: An Interview with Marilynne Robinson." *Face to Face: Interviews with Contemporary Novelists.* Ed. Allan Vorda. Houston: Rice UP, 1993. 153-84.

STUDIES OF HOUSEKEEPING

Aldrich, Marcia. "The Poetics of Transience: Marilynne Robinson's *Housekeeping.*" *Essays in Literature* 16 (Spring 1989): 127-40.

Bachinger, Katrina E. "The Tao of *Housekeeping*: Reconnoitering the Utopian Ecological Frontier in Marilynne Robinson's 'Feminist' Novel." *Für eine offene Literaturwissenschaft: Erkundungen und Eroprobungen am Beispiel US-amerikanischen Texte/Opening Up Literary Criticism: Essays on American Prose and Poetry*. Ed. Leo Truchlar. Salzburg, Austria: Neugebauer, 1986. 14-33.

Bohannan, Heather. "Questioning Tradition: Spiritual Transformation in Women's Narratives and *Housekeeping* by Marilynne Robinson." *Western Folklore* 51.1 (Jan. 1992): 65-79.

Booth, Alison. "To Caption Absent Bodies: Marilynne Robinson's *Housekeeping*." *Essays in Literature* 19 (Fall 1992): 279-90.

Burke, William. "Border Crossings in Marilynne Robinson's *Housekeeping*." *Modern Fiction Studies* 37 (Winter 1991): 716-24.

Cardullo, Bert. "Three Ways to Play House." *Hudson Review* 41 (1988): 348-56.

Caver, Christine. "Nothing Left to Lose: *Housekeeping*'s Strange Freedoms." *American Literature* 68.1 (Mar. 1996): 111-37.

Champagne, Rosaria. "Women's History and *Housekeeping*: Memory, Representation, and Reinscription." *Women's Studies* 20.3-4 (1992): 321-29.

Chandler, Marilyn R. "*Housekeeping* and *Beloved*: When Women Come Home." *Dwelling in the Text: Houses in American Fiction*. Berkeley: U of California P, 1991. 291-318.

Davidson, Lale. "Daughters of Eurydice in Absentia: The Feminine Heroic Quest for Presence in *Housekeeping*." *Journal of the Fantastic in the Arts* 4.4 (1991): 19-36.

Florby, Gunilla. "Escaping This World: Marilynne Robinson's Variation on an Old American Motif." *Moderna Språk* 78.3 (1984): 211-16.

Foster, Thomas. "History, Critical Theory, and Women's Social Practices: 'Women's Time' and *Housekeeping*." *Signs* 14 (Autumn 1988): 73-99.

Galehouse, Maggie. "Their Own Private Idaho: Transience in Marilynne Robinson's *Housekeeping*." *Contemporary Literature* 41.1 (Spring 2000): 117-37.

Gardner, Thomas. "Enlarging Loneliness: Marilynne Robinson's *Housekeeping* as a Reading of Emily Dickinson." *Emily Dickinson Journal* 10.1 (2001): 9-33.

Gernes, Sonia. "Transcendent Women: Uses of the Mystical in Margaret Atwood's *The Cat's Eye* and Marilynne Robinson's *Housekeeping*." *Religion and Literature* 23 (1991): 143-65.

Geyh, Paula E. "Burning Down the House? Domestic Space and Feminine Subjectivity in Marilynne Robinson's *Housekeeping*." *Contemporary Literature* 34 (Spring 1993): 103-22.

Hartshorne, Sarah D. "Lake Fingerbone and Walden Pond: A Commentary on Marilynne Robinson's *Housekeeping*." *Modern Language Studies* 20.3 (1990): 50-57.

Hedrick, Tace. "'The Perimeters of Our Wandering Are Nowhere': Breaching the Domestic in *Housekeeping*." *Critique* 40.2 (Winter 1999): 137-51.

Heller, Dana. *The Feminization of Quest Romance: Radical Departures.* Chapel Hill: U of North Carolina P, 1990.

Inoue, Kazuko. "'Resurrection of the Ordinary': Marilynne Robinson's *Housekeeping*." *Language and Culture* [Hokkaido University] 16 (1989): 143-49.

Kaivola, Karen. "The Pleasures and Perils of Merging Female Subjectivity in Marilynne Robinson's *Housekeeping*." *Contemporary Literature* 34 (Winter 1993): 670-90.

King, Kristin. "Resurfacings of *The Deep*: Semiotic Balance in Marilynne Robinson's *Housekeeping*." *Studies in the Novel* 28 (Winter 1996): 565-80.

Kirkby, Joan. "Is There Life after Art? The Metaphysics of Marilynne Robinson's *Housekeeping*." *Tulsa Studies in Women's Literature* 5 (Spring 1986): 91-109.

Lassner, Phyllis. "Escaping the Mirror of Sameness: Marilynne Robinson's *Housekeeping*." *Mother Puzzles: Daughters and Mothers in Contemporary American Literature*. Ed. Mickey Pearlman. Contributions in Women's Studies 110. New York: Greenwood, 1989. 49-58.

Levin, Jonathan. "Making Shadows in the Dark: *Housekeeping* from Page to Screen." *Vision/Revision: Adapting Contemporary American Fiction by Women to Film*. Ed. Barbara Tepa Lupack. Bowling Green, OH: Popular Press, 1996. 101-26.

Lin, Su-ying. "Loss and Desire: Mother-Daughter Relations in Marilynne Robinson's *Housekeeping*." *Studies in Language and Literature* 9 (June 2000): 203-26.

Liscio, Lorraine. "Marilynne Robinson's *Housekeeping*: Misreading *The Prelude*." *English Romanticism and Modern Fiction*. Ed. Allan Chavkin. New York: AMS Press, 1993. 139-62.

Maguire, James H. "Marilynne Robinson." *Twentieth-Century American Western Writers, First Series*. Ed. Richard H. Cracroft. Dictionary of Literary Biography, vol. 206. Detroit: Gale, 1999. 251-60.

Mallon, Anne-Marie. "Sojourning Women: Homelessness and Transcendence in *Housekeeping*." *Critique* 30 (Winter 1989): 95-105.

Maszewska, Jadwiga. "Ecofeminist Themes in Marilynne Robinson's *Housekeeping*." *American Studies in Scandinavia* 28.1 (1996): 63-69.

Meese, Elizabeth A. *Crossing the Double-Cross: The Practice of Feminist Criticism*. Chapel Hill: U of North Carolina P, 1986.

Mile, Siân. "Femme Foetal: The Construction/Destruction of Female Subjectivity in *Housekeeping*, or Nothing Gained." *Genders* 8 (July 1990): 129-36.

O'Brien, Sheila Ruzycki. "*Housekeeping* in the Western Tradition: Remodeling Tales of Western Travelers." *Women and the Journey: The Female Travel Experience*. Ed. Bonnie Frederick. Pullman: Washington State UP, 1993. 217-34.

—. "*Housekeeping*: New West Novel, Old West Film." *Old West—New West: Centennial Essays*. Ed. Barbara Howard Meldrum. Moscow: U of Idaho P, 1993. 173-83.

Ravits, Martha. "Extending the American Range: Marilynne Robinson's *Housekeeping*." *American Literature* 61.4 (Dec. 1989): 644-66.

Rosowski, Susan J. "Robinson's Politics of Meditation." *Birthing a Nation: Gender, Creativity, and the West in American Literature*. Lincoln: U of Nebraska P, 1999. 177-93.

Rubenstein, Roberta. "Transformations of the Ordinary: Marilynne Robinson." *Boundaries of the Self: Gender, Culture, Fiction*. Urbana: U of Illinois P, 1987. 211-30.

Ryan, Maureen. "Marilynne Robinson's *Housekeeping*: The Subversive Narrative and the New American Eve." *South Atlantic Review* 56 (Jan. 1991): 79-86.

Smyth, Jacqui. "Sheltered Vagrancy in Marilynne Robinson's *Housekeeping*." *Critique* 40.3 (Spring 1999): 281-91.

Sprengnether, Madelon. "(M)other Eve: Some Revisions of the Fall in Fiction by Contemporary Women Writers." *Feminism and Psychoanalysis*. Ed. Richard Feldstein and Judith Roof. Ithaca: Cornell UP, 1989. 298-322.

Stump, David. "Illusionary Flood Formed for *Housekeeping*." *American Cinematographer* 69 (1988): 34-41.

Toles, George. "Sighs Too Deep for Words: Mysteries of Need in Marilynne Robinson's *Housekeeping*." *Arizona Quarterly* 47.4 (Winter 1991): 137-56.

Van Dyke, Annette. "Marilynne Robinson's *Housekeeping*: A Landscape of Discontent." *The Big Empty: Essays on Western Landscapes as Narratives*. Ed. Leonard Engel. Albuquerque: U of New Mexico P, 1994. 147-63.

Weintraub, Aviva. "Freudian Imagery in Marilynne Robinson's Novel *Housekeeping*." *Journal of Evolutionary Psychology* 7 (Mar. 1986): 69-74.

Williams, Gary. "Resurrecting Carthage: *Housekeeping* and Cultural History." *English Language Notes* 29.2 (Dec. 1991): 70-78.

BOOK REVIEWS CITED

Gray, Paul. "Castaways: *Housekeeping*." *Time* 2 Feb. 1981: 83.

Schreiber, Le Anne. "Pleasure and Loss." *New York Times Book Review* 8 Feb. 1981: 14.

OTHER WORKS CITED

Beckett, Samuel. *Endgame*. *The Norton Anthology of English Literature*. Ed. M. H. Abrams, et al. 7th ed. Vol. 2. New York: Norton, 2000. 2472-2500.

Brautigan, Richard. *Trout Fishing in America*. San Francisco: Four Seasons, 1967.

Ferril, Thomas Hornsby. "Time of Mountains." *Westering*. 1934. Ed. Orvis Burmaster. Boise: Ahsahta, 1986. 1-2.

Fiedler, Leslie. *The Return of the Vanishing American*. New York: Stein, 1968.

Hawthorne, Nathaniel. *The Scarlet Letter*. *Collected Novels*. Library of America 10. New York: Literary Classics of the United States, 1983.

Jeffers, Robinson. "Continent's End." *Selected Poems*. New York: Vintage, 1965. 4-5.

Pardes, Ilana. "The Book of Ruth: Idyllic Revisionism." *Countertraditions in the Bible: A Feminist Approach*. Cambridge: Harvard UP, 1992. 98-117.

Pearce, Roy Harvey. *Savagism and Civilization: A Study of the Indian and the American Mind*. Baltimore: Johns Hopkins UP, 1965.

Roethke, Theodore. "My Papa's Waltz." *American Poetry: The Twentieth Century, Volume 2*. Library of America 116. New York: Literary Classics of the United States, 2000. 620-21.

Scheick, William J. *The Half-Blood: A Cultural Symbol in Nineteenth-Century American Fiction*. Lexington: UP of Kentucky, 1979.

Slotkin, Richard. *Regeneration Through Violence: The Myth of the American Frontier, 1600-1860.* Middletown, CT: Wesleyan UP, 1973.

Smith, Eric Todd. *Reading Gary Snyder's* Mountains and Rivers Without End. Western Writers Series 142. Boise: Boise State U, 2000.

Snyder, Gary. "Endless Streams and Mountains." *Mountains and Rivers Without End.* Washington, D.C.: Counterpoint, 1996. 5-9.

Steinbeck, John. *The Grapes of Wrath and Other Writings, 1936-1941.* Library of America 86. New York: Literary Classics of the United States, 1996.

Sten, Christopher. *The Weaver-God, He Weaves: Melville and the Poetics of the Novel.* Kent, OH: Kent State UP, 1996.

Thompson, Morton. *Not as a Stranger.* New York: Scribner, 1954.

Twain, Mark. *The Adventures of Tom Sawyer. Adventures of Huckleberry Finn. Mississippi Writings.* Library of America 5. New York: Literary Classics of the United States, 1982.

Wilbur, Richard. "Sumptuous Destitution." *Emily Dickinson: A Collection of Critical Essays.* Ed. Judith Farr. New Century Views 12. Upper Saddle River, NJ: Prentice-Hall, 1996. 53-61.